PROMISES TO KEEP

Amelia Atwater-Rhodes

PROMISES TO KEEP

DELACORTE PRESS

Published in the United States by Delacorte Press, an imprint of
Random House Children's Books, a division of Random House, Inc., New York.

Delacorte Press is a registered trademark and the colophon
is a trademark of Random House, Inc.

Visit us on the Web! randomhouse.com/teens

Educators and librarians, for a variety of teaching tools,
visit us at RHTeachersLibrarians.com

Library of Congress Cataloging-in-Publication Data is available upon request.

ISBN 978-0-385-74192-7 (trade) — ISBN 978-0-375-99032-8 (glb) —
ISBN 978-0-375-98872-1 (ebook)

The text of this book is set in 12-point Loire.
Book design by Jinna Shin

Printed in the United States of America

10 9 8 7 6 5 4 3 2 1

First Edition

Promises to Keep *is dedicated to the eleventh hour and all the people who help us through it. This novel owes its eleventh-hour salvation to Bri, Mason, and Devon, who had faith and patience when mine was long gone. Bri encouraged me to dive for a story idea that has scared me for the last decade; Mason and Devon helped me polish that concept, tirelessly diving into the characters, mythology, and storyline again and again until it became the book you now hold.*

Two other groups deserve a shout-out: Veterans of the long-abandoned NRPG may find something familiar in these pages . . . and will probably laugh a lot when they recognize it. The idea formed in those crazy days never could have survived without the near madness that is National Novel Writing Month, so I must also tip my hat to the Office of Letters and Light once again.

Next, I also owe huge thanks to the awesome people at Eastern Mountain Sports, who were willing to answer my increasingly bizarre questions about winter backpacking (as soon as I assured them that I did not intend to embark on this poorly planned adventure myself). Any inaccuracies or blatant mistakes should be blamed on magic, not on them.

Finally, it has been too long since I have thanked you, my readers. You ask me all the time where I get my inspiration. The answer is always "You." Thank you.

PROMISES TO KEEP

Whose woods these are I think I know.
His house is in the village though;
He will not see me stopping here
To watch his woods fill up with snow.

My little horse must think it queer
To stop without a farmhouse near
Between the woods and frozen lake
The darkest evening of the year.

He gives his harness bells a shake
To ask if there is some mistake.
The only other sound's the sweep
Of easy wind and downy flake.

The woods are lovely, dark and deep.
But I have promises to keep,
And miles to go before I sleep,

And miles to go before I sleep.

—Robert Frost,
"Stopping by Woods
on a Snowy Evening"

PROLOGUE

MIDNIGHT
SEPTEMBER 22, 1804

WHEN SHE FIRST woke, Brina thought the stench and noise that greeted her were an extension of her nightmares. The stink of smoke and scalded flesh accompanied wails of pain and fear that echoed through Midnight's stone halls.

She had spent the last three days with little rest and less sustenance as she had struggled to put the final touches on a series of paintings illustrating the afterlife. Though her cohorts had always insisted that vampires couldn't *have* nightmares, couldn't have dreams at all, for a century and a half she had dreamt almost every time she had closed her eyes. The diurnal terrors inspired by the Mayan Xibalba had been particularly gruesome.

Another reason she didn't sleep often.

Awake now, she stumbled out of bed. Her body was heavy and her skin raw, a result of too many hours under midday sunlight. Her kind was normally compelled to sleep when the sun was high, but Brina needed the light for her art.

Reality further intruded as she tripped over Caleb, a young boy she had recently taken in, who was huddled against the side of her bed. He must have smelled the smoke, heard the screams.

Despite his youth, Caleb didn't cry or call out; he had been raised not to. But Brina could see him tremble and could smell his sweat in the rising heat. His heart pounded and his lungs strained against the smoke seeping under the room's only door.

In this building, the heart of an empire built by vampires, there were no windows. Brina could have willed herself away in an instant using vampiric magic, but she was not strong enough to bring Caleb with her.

She pulled the door open. Fire, flickering with the pulse of vicious magic, gnawed at the stone walls. The reek of burned flesh gave testimony to how many humans and shapeshifters, some slaves and some willing employees, had been caught trying to flee the pyre.

No escape, not for anyone mortal.

"Come here, boy," she commanded, retreating to the farthest corner of the room.

The boy came to her without hesitation, his wide eyes watering from the smoke but otherwise revealing a placid soul. She snapped his neck before the sweet, trusting look could leave his face.

There. That's done.

She willed herself to her home, where windows let in the sun and—

The stench of death greeted her as she appeared in her own parlor, making her gag. The blood was fresh, but marked by the smell of decay. The instant a body stopped functioning, it began to rot; it took only minutes for this to be detectable to vampiric senses.

The corpses of slaves littered her floors, their eyes wide and their throats slit. They had not died slowly, but neither had their deaths been especially swift. Whoever had done the deed had been efficient, not merciful. Who? *Why?*

"Brina!"

She turned to find her brother reaching for her. His hands and face were slicked with blood and ash. "I couldn't get to you," Daryl choked out as he pulled her into a tight embrace. "I tried to get inside, but every entrance was blocked. Are you hurt?"

She shook her head. "My greenhouse—"

"Gone."

"My paintings?"

"I'm sorry."

"My boy is dead."

"Probably for the best." He pulled her into the next room, where the only evidence of the slaughter was a single crimson handprint on the doorframe.

Meanwhile . . .

Sara Vida had a clear shot.

The Mistress of Midnight, a vampire known as Jeshickah, was undeniably the most evil creature to ever walk the face of the earth. Her empire ruthlessly claimed dominion over vampires, shapeshifters, humans, and witches—though the witches, Sara's kin, were almost an afterthought.

Sara was standing only a few yards from the fiend. The witch gripped a silver knife, imbued with the power of generations of magic-wielding hunters. And Jeshickah was distracted, dazed, staring at the building as it burned to ash, the building that had been the heart of her empire. It would be so easy to sneak up on her and end her unlife.

Sara crept closer, closer, and then paused as the mercenary's words came to mind.

Jeshickah is protected by powers too great for us to fight, the mercenary had warned when Sara had objected to the plan. Why were they destroying property and not killing the fiends who ran this monstrosity? *If you kill her, her allies will come for you. You will not be able to beat them. They will slaughter you, and your children, and your entire line. They will wipe the witches from the face of this earth.*

Could it be true? Midnight had never systematically hunted witches, but it had terrorized Sara's kind nevertheless. By killing Jeshickah, would Sara save her people or ensure their extinction?

Jeshickah tensed, at last sensing the danger.

Too late.

The *sakkri* had given Sara a prophecy just before the attack had begun: *Not all hesitation is sin. Not all sacrifice is in vain.*

As the Mistress of Midnight turned toward her, Sara dropped the knife and closed her eyes. She didn't know whether, generations from now, her kin would thank her or curse her. . . .

If they were alive to do either, that would be enough.

CHAPTER 1

PRESENT DAY

JAY'S ARMS PINWHEELED like those of a cartoon character as he tried to avoid tumbling backward down the cellar stairs. It looked silly, but it gave him enough momentum to throw himself forward instead. When he fell, his shoulder connected with the knee of the vampire, snapping the joint. An extra twist, and she was the one who fell down the stairs.

He heard the impact of bones and flesh on rough concrete—then no more. *Damn.* That meant the vamp had disappeared, and would reappear momentarily to—

You arrogant witch.

The hostile thought from behind Jay gave him warning. He spun around, bringing his knife up as he did so.

The vampire's black eyes widened in surprise as the slender silver blade slipped between her ribs and into her heart. A fall down the stairs hadn't hurt her, but even if the knife hadn't had three centuries of witches' power in the metal, this vamp wasn't strong enough to survive a heart blow.

Jay pulled the knife away, and the late shopkeeper fell back, into a display of faux-Native American souvenirs—plastic dream catchers, miniature tepee tents, and other kitsch that had little connection to the Mohawk people this area was named after. A Santa Claus key chain, one of the few nods to the Christmas season, plunked directly into the pool of blood that welled up around the wound.

Jay started to turn away, then hesitated. It was stupid—his kind didn't even celebrate Christmas—but he felt bad leaving the poor Santa sitting in the quickly drying blood.

He rescued Saint Nick, brushed off the powdery remnants left by vampiric blood turned to dust, and returned him to his fellows on the shelf. Then Jay stretched out his senses.

The storekeeper had been the last of three vampires Jay needed to deal with. One of the others was sprawled at the bottom of the cellar stairs, and the third was draped across the cash register. All of them were now permanently dead. From downstairs, though, Jay could sense the rising panic and hope of the victims he had come to rescue.

What's happening? Is it more of them*? Who are they fighting with? What's going on?* The questions came, rapid and panicked, from two of the three shapeshifters. The third one's mind was sluggish and incoherent. Drugged? Or blood loss?

Jay wiped his knife on his jeans, returned it to its sheath at the back of his neck, and then hurried downstairs, where he found the captives blindfolded, gagged, and bound.

"I'm here to help," he announced as the two conscious shapeshifters flinched from the noise. "SingleEarth sent me."

The SingleEarth organization was a multinational coalition of witches, shapeshifters, vampires, and humans. These three shapeshifters were students at one of SingleEarth's schools. When they had failed to return from a hiking-and-swimming day trip, SingleEarth had dispatched Jay to find them. After all, these woods were Jay's home, even more than the farm his family owned or the room he occasionally used at the local Single-Earth haven.

He had expected to find the shapeshifters lost in the forests of western Massachusetts. He had *not* expected to find them imprisoned by three entrepreneurial vampires who had decided a supply of shapeshifter blood would be a good thing to keep on hand.

Jay pulled blindfolds off and gags down but ignored words of thanks as he turned to the bonds that held the shapeshifters' wrists behind their backs. The vampires had tied each shifter in a way that held a length of rebar against his back, preventing them from shifting and escaping. No shapeshifter could change form with a line of steel next to his spine.

The unconscious shapeshifter's pulse was slow and erratic, and his skin was clammy. He was close to gone. Jay pulled his cell phone out of his pocket and then shook his head as he realized the battery had died . . . probably days ago, while he had been traipsing through the snowy woods. What time was it, anyway? He had a party to get to.

There was a phone and a clock upstairs. Jay was halfway there before the shapeshifters' anxious thoughts caught up to him: *Where is he going?*

"Need to make a call!" he shouted back from the stairs. "Lay your friend down, elevate his feet, try to keep him warm." Jay knew the basics of how to treat blood loss, because a vampire hunter needed to, but he wasn't a healer.

Jerky?

The query came from a Canadian lynx who had been waiting lazily outside the front door. He had helped Jay track the shapeshifters here, but he hadn't had much interest in joining the fight itself.

Lynx had been a cub when Jay had met him two years ago. They had bonded swiftly, and now Lynx's presence meant Jay's senses were sharper—the traditional five, as well as his sense of the fluid shifts in the power around him. In exchange, Lynx's life span would be longer, and his body stronger and more resistant to disease and injury. Hopefully that included resistance to the salt and chemicals that packed beef jerky, for which Lynx had developed a ferocious fondness.

Jay grabbed a strip of moose jerky from a box beside the register and tore it open while he held the store's phone to his ear with his shoulder. It didn't count as stealing when you took things from people who'd tried to kill you, right?

Lynx had eaten two strips before Jay had finished calling SingleEarth for medical support and a cleanup crew. By the time the EMTs had arrived and Jay had sponged blood off his skin in the restroom, he was ridiculously late to hook up with his carpool.

"Sorry, I couldn't wait any longer," the bloodbond said when Jay called to ask if he could still get a ride. "I'm almost there now."

"Damn." A bloodbond was a human tied to his or her vampiric master through a blood exchange, as well as what Jay considered an unhealthy level of emotional dependency. He couldn't expect this one to willingly run late to an event her master considered important.

"Is there anyone else I can get a ride with?" he asked. "I was really looking forward to this bash."

If helping SingleEarth made him miss the best vamp-fest of the year, he was going to . . . whine and do nothing about it, most likely. SingleEarth paid pretty much all his expenses. He was obligated to help them out occasionally.

"Well . . ." The bloodbond hesitated. She probably wasn't supposed to let him know precisely where the house was.

"I would *really* hate to disappoint Nikolas," Jay added. "He asked me to come." Invoking her master's name was dirty, underhanded manipulation. Jay was cool with that.

"I guess I could give you directions?"

"Great! I have a pen right here." Jay knew to accept the offer quickly, and swiped a souvenir pen and a handful of receipts to write on.

Kendra's annual Heathen Holiday was infamous—and extremely exclusive. The celebration lasted from Christmas Eve until New Year's Day and was as much an art exhibition as a social gathering. Kendra's line was primarily made of artists— emotionally unstable, frequently violent artist *vampires*, specifically. No witch and certainly no *hunter* had ever been invited. All the most powerful and influential bloodsuckers would be gathered in one place.

Jay changed into a tux featuring a black silk jacket and a green and gold vest. The cashier at the rental shop had assured him that the color complimented his hazel-green eyes and auburn hair, which he brushed and pulled back into a ponytail.

Want to come to a party? he asked Lynx.

The cat merely yawned.

Lynx would be able to make his way home when he wanted to. Jay double-checked to ensure that his knife was accessible but not visible, then got into his car and eased it onto the snowy road.

He hoped he would get there in time. It would be so disappointing if all the good vamps were gone.

CHAPTER 2

JAY HAD BARELY stepped through the front door of Kendra's mansion, when he stopped dead in his tracks, staring at the larger-than-life sculpture that dominated the front hall.

The artist had captured in blown glass the very instant when a proud huntress launched a falcon from her wrist. Her expression held despair, and hope, and pain, and power, all at once. The falcon seemed like her soul, freed of its earthly bonds. Could she fly with it, or was she forever earthbound, cursed to only dream of the skies?

He saw that his hand had risen, and grabbed his own wrist to stop himself from touching the sculpture. Instead, he reached up as if to casually rub the back of his neck, and let the back of his hand brush the silver hilt of his knife.

A hand like iron closed over his wrist, and another twined in his hair as a melodious voice observed, "You smell of dead blood and adrenaline, witch."

The voice startled him—a sensation he didn't often have, since his power gave him an awareness of others that tended to make it impossible for anyone to sneak up on him. Staring, transfixed, at the statue had been stupid, but how could he have avoided it? Likewise, the mind that flowed over his at that moment made his knees weak. It had to belong to Kendra.

"It's remarkable," he said, struggling to focus on the danger and not the power of her. "As are you."

He didn't mean to say the last bit aloud, but he couldn't help himself. Her mind was like a supernova, full of brilliant colors, swirling fire, and enough gravity to pull entire planets in her wake. What made her thoughts burn with such intensity? Was it always like this, standing in the presence of a mind more than two thousand years old? Or had she always been this way, even before the change?

Kendra mentally responded to both compliments while maintaining a razor-sharp focus on his movements. If Jay struggled, she would snap his neck before he could try for a knife or focus his magic to fight.

"It was his last work," she replied, "and it may be the last thing you see, unless you explain what brings such a pedigreed hunter to our holiday."

He should probably have *started* with that explanation.

"Nikolas invited me," Jay answered. "He hoped he could

convince my cousin, Sarah, to come if she knew someone else here."

Though he had been assured of Kendra's fondness for Nikolas, the emotions Jay sensed from her in response to his name spoke of possession more than affection. Sarah's name barely elicited a blip of recognition.

"I have not seen Sarah. Nikolas left a few minutes ago. And you still smell of blood."

Honesty was a gamble, but Jay wasn't good at bluffing. "That is why I am late."

With her skin touching his, Kendra's thoughts were as clear as fine crystal as she considered what to do with him. Given the importance of her holiday, anyone of any consequence in the vampiric world was currently in this house. That meant Jay couldn't have killed anyone terribly important tonight.

She could kill him just on principle, but Nikolas probably *had* invited him, which meant the laws of hospitality applied.

"Well," she said, slowly releasing first his hair and then his wrist, before taking a step back, "I suppose every cherry tree needs its branches pruned now and again to produce the best fruit."

It took him a moment to realize that she had just given approval to his killing her kind.

Moving his hand away from his knife, Jay turned, and found that the woman standing before him was every bit as regal and elegant as the huntress in the statue. Her lush blond hair and generous figure were showcased in a gown where silver and scarlet dragons cavorted on silk damask.

Of course she wears dragons. No lesser creature could do her justice, Jay thought as he tried to untangle his tongue, focus despite the pure power assaulting his metaphysical senses, and say something intelligent.

"My lady," he managed.

Amused, Kendra held out her hand, which Jay nervously accepted. He kissed the back, feeling slightly foolish but afraid to do anything less.

Meanwhile, she sized him up critically. An hour before, he had thought he looked good. Now he was acutely aware that while the tux fit, it was not a handmade one-of-a-kind item, as Kendra's gown no doubt was.

"Your patron has already left for the evening," she pointed out. "I assume you intend to do the same."

He spoke quickly, words prompted as much by the disdain he could sense from her as by his own intentions. "My invitation might have been for Sarah's benefit, but I was still honored to receive it. Your holiday is famous for its art. I would hate to leave without a chance to take it all in."

She was skeptical, but she was also two thousand years old, and confident in her own immortality. She wasn't afraid of him, or for her guests.

"Enjoy yourself, Jay Marinitch," she said at last. "Mind your manners."

She swept away and left him alone in the front hall, and only then did Jay become aware of the thundering of his own nervous pulse. As his family and other vampire hunters often reminded him, Jay had never been a paragon of common sense.

They would have told him he had to be suicidal to have accepted Nikolas's invitation in the first place, and that it was beyond insane to stay once he'd learned Nikolas was already gone. But in the moments when Kendra's attention had been on him, Jay had been submerged in the most extraordinary aura he had ever experienced. He couldn't stand to go back out in the cold. Not yet.

Instead, he read the plaque at the base of the statue.

LADY WITH A FALCON ON HER FIST

LORD DARYL DI'BIRGETTA

The vampire known as Lord Daryl had been killed two summers ago, an event shocking enough that news had traveled swiftly.

Hunters frequently took down the young and the sloppy, vampires who had been changed by whim instead of thoughtful intent, who had relatively few connections to others of their kind, and who tended to surround themselves with attention-drawing kills. It was far rarer for a hunter to actually strike at the kind of individual who attended Kendra's Heathen Holiday, who had allies, friends, and political connections throughout the vampiric world.

Lord Daryl had not been an ancient, but he had been a powerful figure in his domain, especially in the realm known as Midnight, an empire where humans—and occasionally witches or shapeshifters—had been bought and sold as slaves. When Midnight had fallen two centuries ago, another group had claimed leadership over all vampires and had supposedly outlawed their slave trade, but Daryl was proof that the laws hadn't entirely worked. It was hard for a hunter like Jay to get solid information, but it had become clear in recent years that Midnight had been reborn and was gaining power once again.

Rumors claimed that Daryl's own slave had killed him.

Jay shuddered, turning away from the statue. How could a man known for his viciousness as a trainer, whose career had been dedicated to transforming free souls into broken slaves, ever create such a powerful yet delicate work of art?

Jay caught himself staring again.

Move, Jay.

Beyond the entry, the spectacle was overwhelming. Paint, ink, stone, clay, metal, glass, canvas, photo, paper, wood . . . Thousands of years of talent were showcased here, in every possible medium.

The artistic creations were not the only works of beauty.

The members of Kendra's line, assembled together in full formal wear, were breathtaking. Nikolas had told him the dress code was "more or less black tie," and now Jay understood what "more or less" meant. The vampires and bloodbonds in the room were from every century and every country. Tuxedo jackets and ball gowns moved among saris, mandarin gowns, and other apparel Jay couldn't begin to name.

Beyond clothes, *skin* had in many cases been used as a canvas. Many bloodbonds had been painted, some with elaborate masquerade-style face paint, but others with body art that complemented their attire. One glittering creature wore a dress with an open back that revealed shining painted butterfly wings.

After letting out a squeak of disappointment when the mural he had been admiring moved away to mingle with the other guests, Jay reminded himself that he needed to pay attention to the *people* around him and not just the minds and art.

Kendra alone had been overwhelming. Now Jay was surrounded by such powerful, brilliant minds that it was hard to even see the faces associated with them. In this kind of daze, if someone came at him with a blade, he might just smile at the way the light sparkled on it.

Where am I? He had been wandering, paying no attention, but now found himself surrounded by music and movement.

Colors blended as couples danced in a way Jay had only ever seen in movies, formal patterns responding to the arcing melodies of a string quartet. Standing among them was like standing in a surf, *feeling* the rhythm. He ducked out of the way when a pair nearly spun into him, and he ran into—

Static. White noise.

The mind he faced made Jay feel as though he'd been dunked in an icy lake. Dressed in immaculate black and white, the human before him was apparently one of the help, not a guest. His mind was oddly sterile, still, devoid of emotion or wanting.

"Refreshment, sir?" the servant offered, nodding to the silver tray he carried, which was heavy with glasses of champagne and some unrecognizable finger food—probably caviar, or something equally vile. Jay doubted anyone here cared about underage drinking, but the last thing he needed was alcohol . . . or fish eggs.

"Is there somewhere I could sit for a while?" he asked.

"Yes, sir. This way."

The servant led, and Jay followed with a shiver. It was like walking behind a ghost, something not altogether *there*.

As they entered a quiet parlor, an unsettling thought nudged into his mind: maybe this man wasn't a *servant* at all. After all, Kendra's line was allied with Midnight, the heart of a lucrative slave trade. Though humankind in this country had stopped trading people more than a century before, many immortals had a different sensibility about the uses to which a life could be put.

Midnight's trainers had employed a bevy of methods designed to strip free will and any other vestiges of a soul from those they'd claimed to own, including many of Jay's ancestors. Witches who went to Midnight intending to kill the trainers reappeared like zombies, intent only on obeying their new masters' commands to murder their former kin. Was the static darkness in this servant's mind the result of that same process?

Except for the late Lord Daryl, the trainers were exclusively from one line—all immediately descended from the so-called Mistress Jeshickah herself. Jay dared to hope they didn't share Kendra's line's love of art and so might not choose to attend Kendra's soiree. Even so, the glow of his initial fascination had dimmed, putting him on edge.

Jay found sharks, lions, polar bears, and crocodiles beautiful, each in their own way, but any one of them could turn

into a man-eater given the wrong circumstances, so he tended
to give them a wide berth. Beauty aside, why had he now put
himself in a situation where some of the creatures around him
might want just his blood, but some of them might actually
want his *soul?*

CHAPTER 3

JAY WAS FOOLISH and impulsive at times, but even he wouldn't have come into this crowd alone as a hunter. He also wouldn't have come just to see Sarah—he could see his cousin easily enough in a safer environment. But he might never have another chance to see *this*, the awesome whirl that was thousands of years of artistic talent.

Now that he had tasted the rotten pit in the center of this sweet fruit, however, he needed to move on, before he stumbled across something he couldn't stand to ignore.

He was on his way to the door when his plan was hijacked by a set of paintings.

According to the plaques that accompanied the series, the woman depicted was the Norse goddess Freyja, "a lover, a mother, a witch, and a warrior," who rode at the front of the Valkyries as they collected the souls of the bravest fighters.

Momentarily alone in the room, Jay took in the dramatic, sweeping paintings, some depicting scenes of battle and others explicit enough to make him blush. His drive to leave eroded. He had never known that oil on canvas could be so powerful. As he stared at a depiction of Freyja near her slain husband, it took him several moments to realize that the sorrow he was feeling wasn't coming from paint.

He turned to discover that a woman now occupied the couch he had abandoned. Her elaborate gown was rumpled and stained with paint. Her feet were tucked up next to her, and she laid her head on the armrest. Jay could see bare toes peeking out from her torn skirt hem.

"Are you all right?" he asked, kneeling down to retrieve an ivory hair comb that had fallen next to her. Like the gown and the dark ringlets falling around her shoulders, the comb was streaked with dried paint.

"I'm fine," she lied. She took the comb from him but made no move to place it back in her hair. "I thought no one was in here."

"I was admiring the paintings," he said, "but I'll leave if . . ." He trailed off; his reference to the paintings had triggered a trickle of something other than bone-deep sorrow. "Are these yours?" he asked.

She nodded, and the pinprick of light inside her flared briefly.

"They're . . ." He wanted to bring that light back, but he

didn't have the words he needed to express the way the art around him made him feel.

"They're trash," she interrupted, the spark snuffed. She stood and brushed past him to critically examine her own work. "Tripe hung to please Kendra, or Kaleo, but certainly not me." She lifted a hand to touch the face of Freyja's dead husband before snapping, "Go. Go away."

At a loss, Jay obeyed, though guilt nagged at him for walking away when she so obviously needed *somebody*. If he had known how to comfort her, he would have.

The adjacent room was occupied by a small but rowdy group engaged in an intense debate. There were no servant-slaves among them, though someone had left two plates of appetizers on what was probably a priceless antique table.

Jay leaned against the wall, taking a moment to soak up the friendly atmosphere. This group's energy and enthusiasm felt cleansing after the artist's melancholy.

"I'm only saying," a human man protested as he leaned over the table to swipe a snack from the tray, "that working with Rikai is like working with some kind of venomous animal. She's perfectly lovely right until she tries to *eat* me. I know you two are close, but I must express concern on behalf of your *actors*—myself included."

"Concern noted," the vampire in the middle of the group answered.

Rikai! Jay tuned into the conversation with interest when he heard the name. Rikai was a Triste, a creature who had studied and trained beneath another of her kind and had gained a vampire's near-immortality and a witch's ability to manipulate raw power. She was supposed to be an expert in the study of power of all kinds but was also said to be vicious in her quest for knowledge, willing to exploit anyone who gave her opportunity—except, perhaps, the two others in her elite group.

Given the context, the vampire discussing Rikai had to be Xeke. They were both part of a group called the Wild Cards, a trio of artists whose irreverent works ranged from mildly irritating to frighteningly infuriating. Their third compatriot had once been a witch, like Jay, but had broken those ties long before his birth. Now she was a writer, telling the stories no one wanted her to share. Xeke was supposed to be the most cautious and polite of the three, the one who maintained the greatest number of political and social ties. Jay had never met him but had followed his exploits from a distance.

When Jay made inappropriately intrusive remarks, people called him young and impulsive, unable to control his empathy. When Xeke put the same kind of remarks on film, people called it art. Jay owned several of Xeke's more controversial videos, and had once written a fan letter that he suddenly hoped Xeke had never received.

"Oh, hell, it's late. I've got to run, luv, if I'm going to get back on set in time." The blond human kissed Xeke on the cheek and then darted out of the room, nearly colliding with Jay.

Jay tried not to blush as he felt Xeke's attention turn to him. The vampire stood to greet him with a warm "Welcome" that betrayed both curiosity and interest. His thoughts had a predatory flavor but a neutral tone that Jay tended to find in nature, as opposed to the hostile aggression he associated with most humans and once-humans when they stalked their prey.

"Hi." *Real clever.* He tried to ride the coattails of Xeke's calm-and-collected-ness.

"You look a little overwhelmed," Xeke observed.

"Is any of this art yours?" Jay said, the first polite question he could summon.

"Some of the photos," the vampire answered, "but most of my work is in cinema." He glanced at the clock and remarked, "It's rather late for your kind to be here."

Jay followed the vampire's attention, and realized it was only a few minutes from midnight. Known as the Devil's Hour at gatherings such as this, midnight was traditionally when the vampires fed. Xeke could smell that Jay was a witch. He was intrigued but also distinctly wary.

"Are you asking?" Jay asked.

"Pardon?"

Oh. He had done that thing where he responded to something not said out loud, skipping ahead in the conversation.

Jay reached a little more toward the vampire's mind, getting a more solid sense of him, and asked, "You're Xeke, right?"

"I am," the vampire answered. "And you are?"

"Jay Marinitch."

"A full-blooded witch at Kendra's gala?" Xeke asked, no doubt recognizing Jay's family name. Voice somewhat cooler, he added, "And a hunter, if I'm not mistaken. Surely you aren't intending to do something stupid?"

"I try to avoid stupid things," Jay responded. *Occasionally successfully,* he thought. He was going to get an earful about coming here once Sarah got wind of it. "I'm here as a guest, not to hunt."

"Yet you're armed."

"Of course I'm armed. You can't ask a cat to shed its claws."

"Are you a pet?" Xeke asked, his mood lightening in the face of Jay's honesty. "Or more of a wild animal?"

"Depends on how I'm feeling," Jay replied. Sometimes he was a lizard, or a fox. Sometimes he wanted to be a kitten. "What are you looking for?"

He hadn't intended the words to be flirtatious, but as Xeke quirked one brow and the images in his mind answered for him, Jay knew the vampire had taken them as such. It was hard *not* to flirt with someone whose mind exuded confidence and frank interest.

Aloud Xeke said, "Your knife makes me nervous."

Jay took a step away, and then turned his back on the vampire so it wouldn't be taken as a threat when he drew his knife.

This blade wasn't just a weapon; it was an anchor. Generations of magic imbued in the silver helped Jay ground himself and focus, despite his limited ability to filter what his empathy picked up. Without it, he might still be staring, slack-jawed, at Kendra, lost in her mind.

He could probably live without it for a few minutes.

He flipped the knife around so he was holding it by the blade, and offered it to the vampire.

"Put it somewhere safe, or give it to someone you trust to get it back to me after."

The offer shocked Xeke. Voice laconic but mind nervous, he asked, "Isn't this violating some kind of ancient law?"

Jay laughed, shaking his head. "You're thinking of Vida's line. Mine trusts us to make up our own minds. I know you'll get it back to me."

"How?" the vampire asked.

"I just know."

And he did. There were mysteries in Xeke's mind, but he would honor any deal he made, and any power relinquished to him willingly would never be abused.

"Telepath?" Xeke asked.

Jay nodded.

Empath, actually, but most people didn't know the difference and didn't care. The crucial distinction at the moment was that, while Jay could shield his mind to keep telepathic creatures from reading *his* thoughts, and could protect himself from most magical intrusions, he wasn't very good at shielding against the empathic impressions he always picked up from those around him. Xeke needed to make his mind up, because Jay needed to get out before he completely burned out.

The clock began to toll midnight.

"Well?" Jay prompted.

"Keep the knife," Xeke said. "I don't know you well enough to accept it."

"Want to get to know me a little better?" Jay asked as he returned the knife to its place. He had been on his way out, anyway. He might as well round out the evening with another new experience.

Xeke was said to be of Kendra's line, and though he was nominally allied with Midnight, he was outspoken against the slave trade. He was also politically savvy enough that he wouldn't want to cross SingleEarth and the witches, which meant Jay was probably safe with him.

Probably. Xeke was also known for breaking rules and crossing people who shouldn't be crossed.

"I think it would be best if I ask you to make very clear what you are offering," Xeke said.

Jay tilted his head—a very feline expression of impatient curiosity—as he met the vampire's eyes directly. "I'm offering blood. I'm offering to let you into my mind. Is that clear enough?" Sometimes he forgot that others needed words to make these things obvious to them.

"Clear enough to be irresistible," Xeke replied as he stepped forward and gently grasped Jay's wrist. He wanted to control Jay's dominant hand, the one best angled to draw his knife.

Jay closed his eyes and let the vampire maneuver him into the position he wanted. Unsurprisingly, he had never done this before.

Xeke was firm but not rough, making it clear in the pressure of his grip that it would be best if Jay didn't struggle. Jay relaxed into the restraint.

At the moment when fangs punctured skin and the blood

began to flow, he felt Xeke's mind nudge his. Jay's shields were too good to be penetrated without permission, but he gave that consent, dropping his mental walls so he was as defenseless as a human.

Suddenly—*screaming.*

Jay shoved away from Xeke and ran toward the shrieks of pain, agony, anguish. He raced through the crowd, dodging couples in bloody embraces, until he was once more at the paintings of Freyja.

No one in the crowd approached the artist while she shredded her own work with her nails, leaving bloody trails behind.

The wild madness rising from her made Jay's head spin. *Why had he left her alone?* He looked around, and the question changed to *Why is* everyone *leaving her alone?* Some people stood and stared with bemused curiosity. Others simply walked away.

Xeke approached but then drew back, shaking his head.

She was like an animal with its foot in a trap, desperate to chew off its own leg, and they were all just going to *let* her.

How can they be so callous?

As he approached, the woman snarled and raised her hand to strike him. When Jay dodged the first blow, she gave up and let him pull her back against his chest. He laid his cheek against her matted hair and wrapped his arms around her waist as he tried to project a soothing image into her fractured mental landscape.

"Beautiful lady," he whispered to her, letting himself see her the way she saw herself. "Lovely dear one, beloved night."

She stilled physically in his arms, though her mind continued to struggle. Her shrieks turned to quiet whimpers. She collapsed, sobbing.

"He's gone," she whispered. "He's gone."

"I'm here," Jay whispered, over and over, trying to soothe the woman's utter loneliness. In her head, she walked through a barren wasteland of parched red earth. "I'm here."

CHAPTER 4

TOTAL WASTE, BRINA thought savagely. *Useless drivel.*

Brina had started the Freyja series, inspired by her brother's *Lady with a Falcon on Her Fist,* just before her brother's death. Technically the paintings were excellent. Color theories and compositional techniques were instinctive to her by now, and she could mix media and pigments in her sleep.

But how could an artist do justice to a goddess of passion when she herself *felt* no passion? Brina had painted battle scenes without hope or triumph, lovers with no love. The only painting in the set worth the cost of its oils had been the one of Od, Freyja's slain husband.

She had given him Daryl's face.

She couldn't stand looking at it; she couldn't stand that

everyone else was ignoring it. They all just walked by. Walked past the statue in the hall, walked past the painting, didn't even think to look, because they didn't . . .

Didn't care.

I'm here. You're not alone.

She half heard the voice, but it only made her angrier. That was what *he* had promised. *Put on a pretty dress and a beautiful smile*, Kaleo had said. *You'll feel better when you aren't hiding alone in here.*

She'd tried to do what he said.

She'd dressed. She'd put up her hair.

But at the thought of facing *that* painting, her still blood turned cold in her veins. Impossible. Instead she had fashioned a noose. Strung it from the rafters of her studio. Climbed onto a stool. . . .

"Come away from that," the voice said now. "You don't need to be there."

Who is that?

She opened her eyes.

Ah, the stranger from the gallery.

He was pretty, but his ignorant attempt to compliment those pieces of trash had been almost as infuriating as being cut down from the rafters by a slave who didn't have the good sense to just let her mistress be *alone*. This vampiric curse, which had once seemed so freeing and beautiful, now denied her the right to die.

She should have died with Daryl.

"You really loved him, didn't you?" the stranger murmured as she leaned against him.

He sounded surprised—a tone she had heard too often. A tone like the trainers had, those bastards who were supposed to be experts in manipulation but constantly thought they could belittle and slur her brother, and then turn around and try to woo *her*.

"I'm sorry," the stranger said, his voice softer, more sincere. "I never knew him. What was he like, to you?"

He was my world.

When they had been on the streets, hungry and cold, Daryl had taken care of her. Had insisted she eat even when there was only enough food for one. Had sold himself in any way he'd needed to, so she wouldn't need to do the same. Despite his attempts to keep her ignorant of the sordid details, she knew he had done things that had horrified him—demeaning, illegal, and often dangerous work, which had left him exhausted, bruised, and heart sore.

He'd sworn he would get them a life worth living, no matter what he had to do.

And he had. For more than a century, they had lived as Lord and Lady di'Birgetta. Even when Midnight had burned, and it had seemed like they were certain to end up on the streets once again, he had gathered what was left and kept them comfortable while their world was rebuilt.

"He's gone," she said.

The stranger didn't say much, but he held her tightly, in a way no one had in a long time. The gentle rhythm of his heartbeat and breath formed a lullaby that soothed her panic. At some point, she had turned to hold him back. Now she never wanted to move. If she could just stay right here, like this, she might not fracture into a million pieces.

But . . . where is here? she wondered at last.

She couldn't well recall the moments—perhaps hours— since she'd made the decision to kill herself.

As she lifted her eyes and focused on his face, the stranger said, "I'm Jay."

No, that's all wrong. "You're more of a sparrow, or lark," she said. He had a thick mane of deep auburn-brown hair, smooth skin of a color somewhere between caramel and burnt sienna, and lovely eyes specked and swirled with green, gray, gold, and brown. "Blue jays are cold colors. But you can be a songbird if you want. That's fine."

"Do you know where you are?" he asked.

Kendra's manor. The Heathen Holiday. Several pairs of eyes were fixed on her with varying amounts of concern or annoyance. One of the most concerned was also one of her favorites.

"Exequías," she greeted the Italian vampire. He had first come to work for her as a model, many years ago, when he was still human. Daryl had tried to convince him to stay longer, after his contract had expired, but he had disappeared.

Brina had always regretted that she hadn't been the one who'd changed him.

"I need to borrow Jay for a bit," Exequías said, with the same charming but fake smile that he liked to use for fans and cameras.

Brina held on tighter to her knight, until he let out a grunt that reminded her that he needed to *breathe.* She let go of him reluctantly, and he pulled away to go with Exequías, saying, "My lady, if you'll excuse me."

She nodded. She wouldn't embarrass herself by asking him to stay. He left with Exequías's arm across his shoulders.

No help for it. He was mortal, and mortals at Kendra's Heathen Holiday were there only by coveted invitation from one of her line. If this "Jay" came here with Exequías, then that was who he would stay with for the evening.

She was still watching where they had gone, when Kaleo knelt beside her. Brina glanced up to see Kendra standing in the opposite doorway, probably having sent Brina's maker here to clean up the mess and avoid future drama.

"I'm fine now," she snapped, rising to her feet.

Kaleo caught her shoulders and turned her to face him.

"I see," he said, looking around at the carnage left by her wild fit.

"It's my own work," she pointed out when he crouched to examine the shattered frame of one of the paintings.

"The canvas on some of these is still sound," he remarked. "We'll see if Kendra's staff can repair any of them."

"Don't bother." Kaleo had dragged these pieces from her studio after she had tried to tell him she didn't have anything to display this year.

Despite her protest, Kaleo started handing bits of wreckage to the slaves who materialized at his hands, anticipating his needs.

"Let's get you cleaned up," he said. "I'm sorry I left you alone earlier. I should have realized how much distress you were in." He lifted her hand and examined her fingertips, which were smeared with the coppery dust that remained when vampiric blood dried. Somewhere in her frantic destruction of her own work, she must have torn fingernails and flesh. Those wounds had healed now.

"I would rather be alone." She had embarrassed herself enough for one day.

"Nonsense."

Three and a half centuries ago, his arrogance had drawn her like a magnet drew iron filings. She had fallen helplessly into the well of his charisma, and hopelessly in love. Daryl had warned her that Kaleo's affections were as deep as paint on a canvas, but she hadn't listened. Hadn't *cared*.

Now he brought her back to her home, dragging her like dust in his wake as he blinked out of Kendra's home and reappeared in Brina's living room across town. He shook his head at the doors she had left wide open after she had ordered the slave who'd cut her down out of her sight.

"Do you have a lady's maid?" he asked as he poked through her wardrobe, searching for something more acceptable to wear back to Kendra's gala.

"No," she lied, though of course she did. *That* servant had been a gift from her brother. Brina's whole household would certainly fall apart without Brina's lady's maid. But she had also been the only one with the temerity to cut Brina down earlier, and Brina didn't want to face her just yet.

Kaleo looked at Brina with a familiar expression that asked, *Why must you be so difficult?*

"I don't want to go back to the party," she announced when Kaleo pulled out a crimson sheath dress that was perfectly his taste and absolutely the opposite of hers.

He sighed in frustration. "Brina, I am trying to *help* you. You obviously can't be alone right now."

"I'm better alone than with *you*."

He grabbed her arm when she tried to sweep past him. "Get dressed, Brina. Come back to the party. By the time you get back here, your studio will be repaired and you can pretend none of this ever happened."

Will a clean dress and a canapé bring my brother back, too? she wanted to demand.

No. She knew better than to mention Daryl to Kaleo, who would only use it as an opportunity to twist the knife. Kaleo didn't care about her grief or her dead brother. He cared about his *image*, and the fact that her breakdown reflected poorly on him. Now her "tantrum" was causing him to miss his precious party.

"Believe it or not," she snapped, "playing dress-up and hanging paintings I despise to make *you* feel better is not my priority." If her heart could beat, it would have been pounding with the exhilaration of standing up to him. If only she had done so when he had first swept into her home that afternoon, demanding that she and her art put in an appearance. Though if she hadn't been at the party, she wouldn't have met that intriguing stranger. "Who was Exequías's toy tonight?" she asked, cutting off Kaleo's saccharine retort. "I haven't seen him before."

"If I heard right, he's a witch, and a hunter," Kaleo replied, shaking his head at her abrupt change of subject. "They're better left alone."

Her own laugh was so sudden, so sharp, that it made her jump. "Oh?" she challenged. "And what was the name of that witch *you* wooed, back before Midnight fell? You know the one. You took her from her family. Left behind her human husband and two darling infants . . . mm, Rachel and something. I can't remember the boy's name. How many times did Rachel try to kill you?"

Her words finally hit their mark.

"Fine," he whispered, his temper coming out not in volume or violence but in his words. "Go throw yourself at the witch. If nothing else, I'm sure he can help you kill yourself."

Kaleo disappeared, leaving her to absorb the echo of his words.

I'm sure he can help you kill yourself.

She turned that last sharp retort over in her head, examining it. Before the witch had come to her, she *had* wanted to kill herself.

What had he done to her?

She thought back to her suicide attempt, and shuddered. At the time, it had seemed like the only option. Now the heavy yoke of grief wasn't *gone*, but she could start to see past it, as if the witch's magic had lanced the worst of the poison from her spirit.

CHAPTER 5

"THAT WAS BRINA?" Jay asked as Xeke led him away. The vampire's arm across his shoulders was meant to look possessive, so Brina would let him go. Jay was grateful that it helped him stay upright despite the pounding in his head.

"She tends to conveniently forget that laws such as freeblood status exist," Xeke said quietly as Jay walked with him back to the room where they had first spoken.

Freeblood laws had been an invention of the original Midnight, back in the sixteen hundreds. Humans could be abducted into the empire by anyone's whim, but witches and shapeshifters were given the right to remain free as long as they abided by Midnight's laws.

"Daryl was her brother?" Jay asked, confirming.

"I'm surprised she's noticed he's dead," Xeke answered dryly.

Jay winced. "She has."

"Should I assume this all means you are no longer in the mood to follow through on that delightful offer you made earlier?" Xeke asked.

Jay considered it. He was shaken, having reached too deeply into Brina's madness, and now felt raw and vulnerable.

"Rain check?" He closed his eyes a moment, trying to focus, and felt his body sway.

"Are you all right?" Xeke shifted his arm from Jay's shoulders to around his waist, taking some of his weight. "You look faint."

"I'll be fine. I should head out." He needed to be anywhere else, far away from so many ancient minds pressing against his.

"Are you driving?" Xeke asked.

"Yeah," Jay answered. He didn't want to drive. Should he take Xeke up on the offer to stay at his place, though? "The couch would be fine," he said.

Xeke chuckled, and said, "Why, yes, I do happen to have a couch where you can crash."

"Sorry," Jay said. "I'm unfocused. It's hard to tell what you've said out loud."

"Most telepaths can't read vampires," Xeke said.

"I'm not a telepath," Jay answered. "I'm an empath. Similar talents, different mechanism."

"You can explain the difference to me later," Xeke said.

"For now, you look about ready to fall over." He reached into Jay's jacket pocket to retrieve his car keys. "I'll drive."

"Thanks," Jay whispered.

He took a few steps, and then felt himself being lifted. Jay shut his eyes.

"You are one mellow witch," Xeke observed.

"You're relaxing to be around," Jay replied.

"You're not helping my ego."

"Your ego doesn't need help."

By the time the car had warmed up, Jay was asleep.

He dreamed of the barren wasteland he had found in Brina's mind. As he walked across the scalding sand, his skin started to char, peeling and flaking into black ash like a Hollywood vampire in the sun.

He woke alone on a comfy sectional sofa. A note on the coffee table said:

> *I had to get to a screening. Feel free to stay as*
> *long as you like, and help yourself to anything from*
> *the kitchen. Your car is in the parking lot.*
>
> *–Xeke*

Was the excuse genuine, or had Jay's host left because he wasn't sure how his hunter guest would act once out of Kendra's territory?

Intrigued by this chance to learn a little more about a man he had long admired, Jay began to look around. Instead of a bed, the largest room boasted a bank of three computers, one of which had been left on, with a video camera plugged into it, and was now flashing the message *Import Successful.*

Hoping for a sneak peek at Xeke's next work, Jay pressed Play. The video was raw footage of an interview.

"It's a controversial subject," the woman in front of the camera was saying. She looked vaguely familiar to Jay, but he couldn't place her. "Even today, many serpiente consider Anhamirak and Ahnmik *gods.* People do not like having their gods studied scientifically."

Now Jay recognized her—she was one of the parabiological researchers working with SingleEarth to investigate the history of serpiente shapeshifters. SingleEarth's scientists had established that vampires, most witches, and all shapeshifters had a link to a particular elemental power called Leona, an immortal being of immense power. Scientists were still trying to figure out what made all her magical descendents so different from each other.

"Would you share your theories with me?" Xeke prompted from off-screen.

"Well." The researcher fidgeted a moment, and then seemed to recall that she was on camera. "Serpiente myth describes a time when they possessed incredible magic, which was wielded by the priests and priestesses of a group called the Dasi. Oral tradition tells of a creature named Leben who tried to take over the Dasi by impersonating their god. The Dasi's leader seduced Leben, and to win her favor Leben gave them all their second shapes." She paused, and with a shrug explained,

"Unfortunately, this 'gift' triggered a series of natural disasters that nearly wiped out the civilization. Hundreds, maybe *thousands*, of the new shapeshifters died in the upheaval, a horrific number when you consider that we're talking about a predynastic Egyptian village, not a modern city."

"You say 'natural disasters.' Were they natural, or magical?"

"Well." That word seemed to be her method of pausing to gather her thoughts. "We know now that Leben is one of Leona's creations. He is directly responsible for the genesis of every shapeshifter living today. My theory is that the serpiente gods Anhamirak and Ahnmik were actually elementals, just like Leona. Like all their kind, they gain power through their mortal bonds. When Leben claimed their worshippers for Leona, Anhamirak and Ahnmik fought back. Either Leona deliberately started killing the new serpiente to weaken their elementals or the serpiente's deaths were a natural consequence of elementals fighting. An earth elemental gets angry, and you get an earthquake—that kind of thing."

"Why would Leona challenge another elemental in the first place?" Xeke asked.

"These days, Leona is unrivaled in power, with thousands of bonds. Back then? As far as we know, she had three vampires, and a small band of witches with nowhere near the power that the serpiente attribute to their ancestors. Leona may have worked through Leben to eliminate the competition."

Ancient immortal soap operas, Jay thought, imagining a reality television show in which a bunch of elementals were trapped on an island together. Chuckling, he stopped the video and went looking for the rest of his belongings.

He found his jacket, tie, and vest hung carefully on a coat-rack by the front door, with his shoes beneath them. Xeke had apparently decided he shouldn't sleep in his full monkey suit and noose.

Noose. The image of Brina dangling with a broken neck, unable to move until one of her slaves cut her down, rose into his mind once more. Jay had seen plenty of violence in his past, but he had never experienced such a black gulf of emotional pain as had driven Brina to try to destroy herself. Delving so deeply into her mind had forced him to feel it the way she did. To feel *himself* swinging there.

He shivered as he stepped out the front door.

He was in a small apartment complex, set well back from the road and backed up against the forest. Tasteful white lights on the trees out front reminded Jay that this was Christmas Day, or would be once the sun rose.

His car was nearby, and a quick check of the GPS made it clear he was across town from Kendra's gala. Few vampires were powerful enough to bring other living creatures with them when they did their teleportation trick, and even for those who could, it was a rough trip for both parties. The lack of bedroom made it clear that this wasn't Xeke's only or primary home; he had probably dropped Jay here because it was the shortest drive.

Jay was a little stiff from sleeping restlessly on a couch, but a short walk would fix that. He liked trees.

But there was something . . . odd . . . about this forest.

He hesitated at the edge of the woods. It wasn't the fact that he was in dress shoes and tuxedo pants, anticipating trudging through the snow. It was . . .

Something.

Yet something else pulled him forward, and Jay Marinitch wasn't one to resist the call of unnamed, unidentified forces suggesting he wander into a dark and unfamiliar forest.

The woods were beautiful, illuminated by the moonlight trickling through naked branches to bounce off the snow beneath. What surprised Jay was the lack of animal tracks. The snow had fallen two days before. Why weren't there signs of foxes, rabbits, and deer?

When he finally *did* sense life, he pursued it.

What he found, curled in the snow, was a woman with skin and hair the color of the night sky, and white streaks like moonlight in her hair. She wasn't sleeping, but neither was she awake. She was just lying in the snow, in a long gown covered in frost.

Her breathing was barely more perceptible than her hypothermic thoughts. When Jay knelt and set his fingers to her throat, he felt that her pulse was steady. He touched her arm, and a whisper of magic replied. A shapeshifter of some sort? That would be good. Shapeshifters were very sturdy.

He put a hand over her heart and slowly trickled warmth into her body, wondering who she was and what might have brought her to be here like this.

Most breeds of shapeshifter had certain defining features.

The Mistari-tigers were of African-Asian descent. Serpiente tended toward dark hair with fair skin. The lions were black in human form, but this woman wasn't just black in the way that humans were; she was actually *black*, like coal. Lynx would have been able to guess her breed by her smell, but Jay couldn't.

She stirred slightly, moaning.

Jay tried to reach for her mind, but it fluttered away, as elusive as a faerie.

As he continued to pour warm power into her, he sensed her body remembering injuries both recent and from long ago. There was a sense of resignation in her flesh, and a memory less substantial than scars that remembered cut and burned flesh, broken bones, blood flowing.

And an even deeper agony.

Suddenly, that agony lashed out at Jay.

He staggered backward and thudded into the snowdrift behind him. His connection to the shapeshifter had been completely severed.

Wind whipped through the forest, making the trees shiver and groan in sympathy. The air rippled like heat rising from pavement. A force whispered to him, *She must come home.*

The force that spoke was . . . maybe not malevolent, but maybe so. He knew only that it was powerful, and it had stopped him from helping the woman.

She can't go home if she dies here, he thought.

He lifted her gently in his arms. If he couldn't keep her warm with his magic, he had to find another way. He wished he hadn't locked Xeke's door behind him. He arranged her in the backseat of his car, wrapped in an emergency blanket. He wanted to call SingleEarth's healers for advice, but his cell phone was still dead. The best he could do was turn on his GPS and ask it to take him to the closest SingleEarth Haven, which was #2.

Perfect; his cousin Caryn Smoke worked at the clinic attached to #2. Caryn was twenty, just a year older than Jay, and hadn't yet finished her formal medical training, but she was already one of the best magical healers he knew. He had recently received an engagement announcement from her, though he couldn't remember who she was marrying, or when. Hopefully it hadn't been a Christmas wedding. He wasn't sure what would become of the shapeshifter if Caryn wasn't there to help.

CHAPTER 6

HE REACHED SINGLEEARTH shortly after dawn, while the winter sky still had that gray-and-purple tone, as if it weren't sure if it wanted to stay dark, get bright, or catch on fire.

After pulling up to the main entrance, Jay left his car running while he went inside to get help. The shapeshifter's body temperature had returned to normal during the trip, but he still hadn't been able to wake her, which meant this was a case for doctors and witches trained in healing, instead of a hunter with a rudimentary knowledge of magical and mundane first aid.

"Can I help you?" the receptionist asked as Jay looked around, hoping to find Caryn loitering conveniently nearby.

"I have a woman in my car out front," he answered. "She's a shapeshifter, she's unconscious, and I can't wake her."

The receptionist pressed a button on her desk and said, "Medical needed at main entrance." Two of SingleEarth's EMTs appeared within moments. The receptionist echoed what Jay had just told her, looking at him only to ask, "What breed?"

"Not sure. You need a witch to look at her, though."

"Bring her in," the receptionist told the EMTs. To Jay, she added, "We have plenty of trained doctors on staff. If it looks like she needs magical care—"

"Where's Caryn?" he interrupted. Jay had napped a couple hours at Xeke's place, but he still needed real *sleep*, of the variety that he liked to regularly engage in for six to eight to twelve hours. He didn't have patience for a bureaucratic runaround from a receptionist who normally dealt with things like shapeshifter obstetrics, minor human injuries and illnesses, and noncritical mystical mishaps.

Winter Village, her mind answered, as she said, "Ms. Smoke is not—"

"Never mind." Though few shapeshifters and fewer witches celebrated Christmas, enough SingleEarth members did that Haven #2 had set up a "Winter Village" in the events hall.

Sure enough, Jay found Caryn there, arranging brightly wrapped presents around a half-dozen evergreen trees whose piney scent had filled the large room. While Caryn meticulously adjusted wrapping and ribbons, her mind raced through thoughts of schedules, dance lessons, and food. Something about a caterer and cake.

"Caryn?"

She turned with an expression that was half smile and half frown. "What's up?" she asked.

"Medical needs you," he said.

"They haven't paged me."

"Trust me."

"Jay . . ." Caryn shook her head and bit back an explanation of *why* the triage process Jay was trying to circumvent existed. Caryn was the only witch regularly at this haven. If she were called for every skinned knee and headache, she would never have time to sleep or eat. "Fine," she said. "What's the issue?"

She followed him toward the medical wing as he explained.

"Was she with the others you called in earlier?" Caryn asked as she waved aside the triage nurse and started checking the shapeshifter's vitals. Pulse was steady, though slow. Breathing even. Temperature slightly elevated for human norms but well within most shapeshifter norms.

"No. I went to a Christmas party and stayed with a friend after." And Kendra's house was . . . hmm. The name of the town was on the tip of his tongue. "Well, I found her in the woods, a bit ago."

"Which woods?" Caryn asked.

Behind the apartment complex, which had been named . . . nope.

"I'll have to get back to you on that," he answered.

Caryn took a deep breath, mentally counting to ten, before she said, "Well, she's in good hands now. Why don't you go get some sleep? Your usual room is empty."

Finally—permission to *sleep*! Jay didn't need to be told twice. He picked up the key at the front desk, stretched out on the sun-streaked bed the moment he entered his room, and then let his mind settle into the shape of *cat*.

His body didn't change, but mentally he was *cat*. A house cat, who lived only to laze about in the sun and be pampered. And one of the things cats liked most was to sleep long, *long* hours, which was why *cat* was one of Jay's favorite things to be.

The Jay-cat dreamed of forests. Of pouncing on butterflies and stalking motes of dust as they drifted in the warm air. Bit by bit, though, he realized something bigger was hunting *him*.

He crouched low, trying to hide. He swiveled his head slowly, looking around, but couldn't find the source of his unease.

Grass rustled like bones creaking back to life. The rocks themselves groaned in response, making his body ache and his skin twitch. He growled.

He woke grumpy, sore, and more tired than he had been before his nap. His sunbeam had left with the morning, his headache had returned, and he knew the mysterious shapeshifter from the woods was somehow responsible.

Jay had too much magic to mistake outside power for a mere dream. Something was trying to communicate with him, something powerful enough that even in cat form, his unconscious mind had instinctively wanted to hide.

Well, whatever it was had ruined his attempt to sleep, which as far as Jay was concerned was a hangable offense.

Hanging.

He still couldn't get Brina out of his head. Could this dream have been a manifestation of her pain, or an impression from the mind of someone else he had encountered at Kendra's? His dreamscapes often echoed lingering bits of the strongest minds he encountered.

No. Vampires didn't rattle him like this. This was something more powerful, more alien.

His stomach rumbled. Still lost in a strange jumble of kitty and witch thoughts, he sought the kitchen.

To a cat, scents were more powerful than sights, and the scents in SingleEarth were always exciting. There were humans and witches and shapeshifters of every kind. Some SingleEarth havens were huge complexes where hundreds of individuals lived, but Haven #2 was small, just a few buildings. Residents mostly cooked for themselves.

People said hello as he opened the refrigerator, trying to figure out if there was something he could make quickly and easily.

Bacon . . . *mmm*, that had promise.

He tossed four strips into a frying pan and turned the knob on the stove, listening for the *click-whump* sound of the gas going on.

As he waited for the bacon to begin crackling, a nagging feeling at the back of his neck whispered to him, warning, *There is something out there, something* big. *It's creeping up behind you, and you're making bacon?*

Food is important, he thought, trying to reason with his own mind.

Survival is critical.

Okay. Fine. He would look in on the shapeshifter, see how she was doing, and maybe figure out the stupid mystery of the ominous lurking power. Maybe she was a hyena or lion or some other predator that his cat mind had sensed and blown out of proportion in his subconscious?

Jay lay his bacon on top of some napkins and carried it with him as he returned to the medical building. The strange shapeshifter was being examined by a human doctor whose mental patter gave him away as Caryn's fiancé. Underneath his forethoughts, which were mostly concern for the still-unconscious woman, he had dance steps on the brain. What was it about dancing?

"Have you tried asking the serpiente?" Jay suggested.

The human jumped, spinning around. "What?"

Why did so many of his conversations begin with people asking, *What?*

"About dancing. You and Caryn are both so stressed about it. Why don't you ask the serpiente? They've danced professionally for thousands of years."

"Thanks, but we're going for a more traditional—I mean, traditionally human—well, traditionally— We're not going for serpiente style dancing, um . . ." He trailed off when he realized he didn't know who he was talking to.

"I'm Jay Marinitch," Jay provided. "We've met, but only once." Jay wouldn't have had the foggiest idea what this young doctor-in-training's name was, either, if it weren't for the convenient name tag reading *Jeremy Francisco, Medical Assistant.* "How is she?"

"Nervous enough to shatter," the human answered with a shake of his head. "We're supposed to go by my mother's this afternoon—for Christmas, you know. It's the first big family event Caryn's come to, and—" He broke off, looking sheepish. "You meant the patient, didn't you?"

Jay *had* meant the patient, yes, but now— "You don't really think they'd *hurt* her, do you?"

"*What?* No, I . . . Wait. Jay. I remember you now," he said, thinking, *Caryn was right. He is always this way.* "One of my uncles had a bad run-in with a shapeshifter psychopath a long time ago, and now most of my family is of the opinion that not-human equals *bad*. When I first told them I was in SingleEarth and marrying a witch, a lot of them talked big and bad. Some of the worst of that still goes through my mind when I'm worried, but I would *never* bring her anywhere I thought she would be in danger."

"Physical danger isn't the only kind," Jay pointed out.

"Right. But, see, this holiday is my mother's big effort to show her support before the wedding. If we don't go, we might as well write off my whole family, and I'm not willing to do that as long as they're halfway trying. I already told my mom flat out that if anyone gets nasty with Caryn, we're leaving."

Jay knew he was a little late to take on the role of big brother. Time to change the subject.

"So, how is the patient?" he asked.

Jeremy's frustration with his parents blended seamlessly with his frustration with this patient. "Physically, we can't find anything wrong with her. Even magically, Caryn says she is stable now. I was about to hit the library, to see if I can identify her breed or where she might have come from. Want to help?"

"No, thanks," Jay said automatically. He could read just fine, but given a choice, he preferred not to. Books were just words to him, flat and static and frustratingly slow to reveal themselves.

"Okay. I'll let you know if I learn anything," Jeremy said. "Mer—um, have a good day."

"Thanks. Merry Christmas," Jay answered, since Jeremy apparently celebrated that holiday. Most of Jay's kind didn't, though some had picked up some neo-pagan leanings and had started claiming holidays celebrated by human witches in the last few decades.

Once Jeremy had left, taking his anxiety and wedding obsessions with him, it was easier for Jay to focus on the other mind in the room. If the problem wasn't medical or magical, then it was probably psychological. That meant Jay was better equipped to deal with it than the doctors. It was silly that they hadn't asked him yet.

Skin-to-skin contact made mental contact stronger. Jay reached out to take her hand.

Yes, the shapeshifter slept, but not in any normal or healthy way. In sleep, people's minds still worked. Even when they didn't dream—even if they were medically brain-dead—they let off sparks from unformed thoughts and neurological impulses. A telepath might hear nothing unless the person were dreaming, but Jay could pick up on the basic static that was *life*.

This woman's mind was as silent as a corpse's. Either there

was absolutely nothing happening in her mind, in which case her body systems should have stopped, or else something very powerful was keeping Jay out.

Normally, he would have taken that as a challenge to which he must rise, but this time he hesitated. Back in the woods, this had gone badly, and he couldn't help but remember the presence that had stalked him in his dreams. Did he *want* to seek this woman's mind?

CHAPTER 7

"JAY, QUIT IT."

The sharp words came from a familiar voice and mind just as Jay had steeled himself to reach for the shapeshifter's hidden psyche.

He drew back carefully from the shapeshifter before standing with a long stretch of his spine and saying, "Hi, Vir. What are you doing here?"

Vireo didn't bother to answer the question, or to continue addressing Jay in any way. SingleEarth had called him to check on their patient, since he was a practiced mental healer. He didn't bother to say anything out loud, because he knew that as soon as Jay asked the question, the answers came to mind. Speaking was a waste of time.

After all, they were brothers.

"Careful," Jay said. "There was another power in her when I first found her. I'm not sure if it was hers, or someone else's, but it threw me out. Hard."

Jay spoke out loud because Vireo, despite having worked most of his life to focus his empathic abilities, wasn't always great at picking up all the details.

Vireo nodded and said, "Thanks," though he had already focused his attention on his patient and was just waiting for Jay to go away and stop being a distraction.

As Jay turned to leave, he heard Vireo's mental suggestion: *You might want to change your clothes, too.*

Oh, right. He was still wearing wrinkled, water-stained tuxedo pants and a dress shirt that had seen better days, and he had never bothered to put his shoes back on after his interrupted nap.

Jay kept a cache of clothes in his car for whenever he ended up somewhere unexpected—which was most of the time. Unless he was hunting, Jay tried not to plan anything more complicated than naps and breakfast, which meant he didn't maintain an apartment. Even his car was registered in his father's name. He was willing to rise to the occasion when he needed to do his job, but he refused to join the stable grind of so-called respectable life.

While he was retrieving his duffel bag from his car, he noticed his dead cell phone on the passenger seat. He brought it with him back to his room and plugged it in before he changed.

Once he was comfortable in jeans and a T-shirt under a heavy sweatshirt he wasn't entirely sure was his, he turned on his phone and dialed into his voice mail.

The first two messages were from Nikolas.

"Marguerite told me she saw you at Kendra's but that she lost track of you. I wanted to make sure you made it home all right."

The second message still sounded calm, but the words suggested otherwise. "Jay, I know you well enough to guess that you are likely to forget about your phone, but do me a favor and confirm you're alive before I need to tell your cousin that you went missing from an event I invited you to."

The third message was from Sarah herself. "Hi, Jay. This is Sarah. Nikolas just told me you showed up at Kendra's bash and apparently left with someone called . . . Xeke? Nikolas assures me this Xeke is as trustworthy as a vamp can be, but you know I want to hear your voice. Call me."

Sarah had been a Vida witch, which meant she was a vampire hunter born and bred. Jay had never caught the whole story of how she had become a vampire, but it was obvious that her change hadn't eliminated her natural distrust of most other vampires.

Jay called and left a message with a bloodbond, who informed him that it was just past noon and that Sarah—like any vampire changed barely two months before—was asleep.

Tag, Sarah. You're it.

With that responsibility attended to, the mystery of the woods needled him like a porcupine quill. His failure to re-

member where he had found the shapeshifter wasn't just a matter of his being absentminded. It suggested magic, which would
best be investigated by a witch.

Of course, Jay *was* a witch, but for this he needed someone
with a specific skill set.

As Jay crept back into the patient's room, wishing he didn't
need to ask for his brother's help, Vireo swore. His attempts
weren't working. Her mind was just too far away, or maybe too
well shielded.

Aware that Vireo had a temper, Jay approached with some
caution before saying, "Are you sure I can't help?"

Vireo wanted to say no. He was sure his brother could reach
the woman, but Jay had no training as a mental healer. It was
kind of like sending a random person with a bullhorn to keep
someone from jumping off a roof. Sure, they would be loud
enough, but they were just as likely to push the person off the
roof as counsel them to safety.

"Can you just tell me if she's in there at all?" Vireo asked.

"She's in there, somewhere," Jay answered. "There's just
something very, *very* wrong with her." Realizing that he could
approach his problem as an offer *to* help instead of a request
for help, he said, "I think it might be related to the woods
where I found her. They were strange, too. But I can't remember where they were, or where I was, or how I got back
here."

Vireo wasn't so deaf that he didn't pick up that when Jay
said *I can't remember,* he meant a vast-enough failure to indicate
a problem.

"Come here," Vireo said. "Sit in front of me."

Jay sat cross-legged in front of his brother, who mirrored his position and then reached out to touch fingertips to Jay's third eye, the spot between the brows where mystics said there was a power center. Jay had never been big on that philosophy; he didn't bother with power points and—

He yelped as Vireo shocked him with a spike of power, a teasing chastisement in reaction to Jay's thoughts. Vireo liked power centers, philosophy, and mojo.

"How did you get to the woods?" Vireo asked.

Jay wasn't being asked to respond out loud. He thought about the party, and the conversation with Xeke. He felt Vireo try to squash a critical thought about his hunter brother offering his throat to a vamp, probably out of an impulse toward professional courtesy.

Jay recalled waking up at Xeke's and walking into the woods from there.

Why did you go into the woods?

Something called me.

Vireo poked around at that memory a little longer, drawing out anything Jay could remember about the trees and the snowdrifts and even the angle of the moon, before asking how he got to Haven #2.

Jay remembered the car. Putting the shapeshifter in. Wrapping her in the blanket. Wondering what time it was. Leaving the parking lot. Driving down a little road . . . and being at SingleEarth.

No matter how much pressure Vireo applied, there simply wasn't anything between the dark, winding road and Single-Earth Haven #2.

"Whatever muddled your mind did a fine job of it," Vireo said as he withdrew from Jay's thoughts. *And the last thing you need is for your brain to get more scrambled.* He asked, "Are you willing to try to reach her again?"

He was still skeptical of letting Jay involve himself with this patient, but anything that had tossed Jay out of the shapeshifter's mind the first time would be far too powerful for Vireo to fight his way past.

"I can try," Jay answered. He was a hunter. He frequently risked his neck, when it was called for.

Jay sat beside the sable-skinned shapeshifter and reached toward her.

Empathy was different from telepathy in one simple way: direction.

Telepaths heard thoughts that others projected. Weak telepaths could only hear the thoughts that someone else had the power to focus and put out into the ether. With proper training, many witches and some shapeshifters were able to develop basic telepathy.

Powerful telepathy, the ability to read and speak to others' minds, was rare among mortals but common among vampires. Mortal blood gave vampires a solid form, but otherwise they—like the elementals who gave them their power—were nothing but raw *force* given sentience. They were creatures of thought, and so they were masters of that realm.

Because it was conscious, telepathy could be blocked through mental effort. Many individuals learned how to guard against it. Empathy was completely different.

Every creature in the world was somewhat empathic. Emotion and instincts were constantly projected in each creature's aura. Individuals who could shield their minds from the most powerful telepaths in the world tended to be naked in front of Jay.

Figuratively speaking.

He hadn't ever had to *fight* to get into someone's mind, the way he fought now. It was like the strands kept slipping away from him, hiding.

Where are you? he wondered, dropping his own mental walls in the hope that he could slip into her mind like a drop of water into a pool.

By the time Vireo yelped *"Jay!"* he was gone, absorbed into a deep, dark forest that received him like a hostile stranger.

Is this a dream? he wondered. The power to walk through others' dreams was incredibly rare, and beyond even Jay's abilities. *If this isn't a dream, what is it?*

The woods were so dark, he was only vaguely aware of tree trunks around him, the black night pressing in . . . and *something* prowling. He couldn't reach out to the beast mentally because he was already *inside* someone's mind, and there wasn't a separate mind in here to reach for.

When he tried to walk on the forest floor, brambles ripped at his legs.

If this was like a dreamscape, he might be able to control it. Could he go up?

Jay let himself be a bird.

When he did this in the real, waking world, the experience was only mental. He formed a connection to the animal and studied its thought patterns until he could slip into them at will. In this world . . . he spread white and blue wings and aimed for the tops of the trees.

Something yanked at him, knocking him back down, until his feathers tangled in the brambles. Thorns like daggers pinned him in place, a warning not to move.

The wind whispered to him as he struggled:

Stay still. Stay silent. Stay still. Stay silent. Do not be.

Not be.

Nobody.

Be nobody. Quiet. Silent. Still.

He couldn't help himself; he struggled, and the brambles savaged his feathers.

Stop fighting! He'll hear you!

Who is "he"?

The wind went silent.

Jay needed to be something sturdier.

He had to slow down. He had to be so patient. He had to wait and gather his shell.

The turtle fell through the brambles, tossed this way and that, but he hid inside his armor until he hit the ground beneath the lowest spines.

It was cold down here, making him even slower, but that was fine.

The turtle was cautious.

The turtle could wait.

He lumbered, seeking something different in the darkness . . . but found only deeper darkness, choking night . . . silence. . . .

CHAPTER 8

"JAY?"

He leaned toward the voice.

"Jay, wake up or I'm going to kill you."

Jay followed the voice—which was as much magic as sound—back toward his brother. When he opened his eyes, he found Vireo looking pale and shaken, and Caryn flushed with relief.

"How long was I out?" he asked.

No one answered him. They probably assumed they didn't need to. But he got nothing. He couldn't hear a thing anyone wasn't saying.

Unsettling.

They were both staring at him, waiting for him to say something.

He wasn't with the shapeshifter anymore but in another SingleEarth medical room, where he had been given a bed of his own. He tried to push himself up, and realized that he was hurt.

"Be careful," Caryn said. "I couldn't heal it all. Your magic fought back when I tried."

The clothes he had been wearing earlier were gone, replaced by light cloth pajama pants like those they gave out in hospitals. He didn't have a shirt on, and there were bandages on his chest. And not just bandages but *stitches*, holding together wounds in the meat of his chest and shoulders.

He remembered the thorns cutting into him. Though the brambles themselves may have been an illusion or fantasy, they apparently represented a real, physical attack.

"What happened?" Vireo asked.

"I don't know. How long was I unconscious?"

"A couple hours," Vireo answered. "I called for Caryn's help when I couldn't reach you mentally and you started to bleed. It took us about an hour to get you stabilized. I take it you're pretty mind-deaf right now?"

Jay nodded. He was too exhausted to hear anything specific in the noise around him, like listening for a whisper after spending hours in a noisy nightclub. Whatever he had touched minds with, it was far bigger than any shapeshifter.

"So . . . ," Vireo said. "I hate to ask while you're still in your sickbed, but did you learn anything useful about our other patient?"

Jay paused to reflect on his experience.

"There is someone, a 'he,' that she is afraid of. I think her being unconscious may be a way of hiding from him. She has an elaborate trap in her mind set up to keep her hidden. I got caught in it when I tried to find her."

"We should probably let Jay rest," Caryn interjected. "Jay, do you need anything?"

He shook his head. He knew someone who might know more about their mysterious patient, but there was no point in explaining his intent to Caryn and Vireo. They would want him to be careful, by which they would mean, "Stay in bed and don't go seeking flirtatious vampires." Considering how many semi-legal and life-endangering escapades Caryn had engaged in, Jay resented her belief that *he* should be careful . . . but he knew better than to challenge her.

Thankfully, Vireo not only *could* shield himself against others' thoughts in a way Jay had never been able to, he considered it polite to do so, so he didn't hear anything inconvenient, and Jay didn't get any comments from either of them on his decision to find Xeke again.

Jay didn't have a choice. He had found the shapeshifter behind Xeke's apartment. Xeke might know who she was.

Besides, it would be fun to see him again.

"I'm good."

Vireo squeezed his shoulder on the way out. "I was worried about you," he admitted.

Jay shrugged, not sure how to respond. "I'm okay," he said.

"Yeah. But I'm the one who asked you to do it, and, well, just be careful with yourself."

With that said, Vireo left quickly. For a man who had dedicated his life to meddling with others' minds, Vireo wasn't comfortable with his own emotional insides.

Once alone, Jay used the phone by his bed to call a Single-Earth secretary, who told him that they had no direct contact information for Xeke but suggested that he try the vampire's club, a place in Boston called The Market.

Information offered two phone numbers matching that description. The first seemed to belong to a clothing store. The other was the club's answering service, which informed Jay that the phones were not manned in the mornings and that he could either leave a message or call back after six.

A few words into telling whoever heard it to ask Xeke to call him, it occurred to him that the message he had been about to leave wasn't going to work.

Hello, this is Jay Marinitch. Xeke and I met last night at a party.

Given the way Xeke liked to flirt, that probably applied to a *lot* of people. The club wasn't likely to give out Xeke's number to every person who called, or to even bother to pass on a message. Jay tried to think quickly. What would actually seem important enough to get them to bother Xeke with it?

"Hi, this is Jay Marinitch." Instead of referring to the party, he said, "I'm in the hospital, and I need to get in touch with Xeke, but I don't have his number with me. He can call me at . . ." He looked over and read out the number posted next to the phone. *Hospital* was a bit of an exaggeration for Haven #2's clinic, but if anyone looked up the number, at least it would come up as a medical facility.

Jay hung up the phone, discovering in the process that his arm was incredibly heavy. He was exhausted. It was time for some good old-fashioned non-coma-style sleep.

He closed his eyes. What should he be? Kitten? Squirrels and bats slept well, too.

Jay couldn't find the energy to shift his mental state to anything other than "bed-bound, injured human-shaped person."

And so as such, he drifted back to sleep.

Not here again.

The brambles and branches menaced, grabbing at him with their needlelike fingers. As he struggled to focus, to become something that would be safe in this hell, the world around him went soft, like a video blurring out of focus.

This is just an echo, he thought. He was in his *own* mind. That meant he could control it, explore it. Understand it.

He slipped through the brambles like a shadow, drawing no attention, and at last found himself outside a tall black fence with iron ravens on the top. He should have been able to see through the gaps in the fence, but there was nothing but darkness.

He walked the length of the fence, trying to find an opening, but there were no corners or gates, no matter how far he walked. He turned around, but instead of the forest, the fence was behind him as well. No matter how he turned, he faced cold iron, blocking his way.

He woke to find Xeke sitting in the chair by his bed, reading a celebrity gossip magazine dedicated to the most ludicrous lies imaginable. Xeke didn't give the tabloids a lot of credit for accuracy, but they certainly were entertaining.

Oh, good. Jay's empathy was starting to come back.

"Good to see you awake," Xeke said. "I was surprised when my secretary passed on your message."

"You have a secretary?"

"I have several."

"I can't remember the name of the town where Kendra's gala and your apartment were," Jay said. "Or how I got back."

"How odd," Xeke said, in a tone that made it clear it wasn't odd at all.

His mind told Jay why. The town was spelled. Not all of it; normal humans lived in enough of the town that it would be terribly awkward if they couldn't remember how to get home or to work or how to give people directions to visit them. But crossing certain boundaries would trigger the spell, which was powerful.

"You seem like an interesting guy," Xeke said, "but I'm surprised it didn't give you even a moment's pause that I would willingly bring a hunter to a place where I routinely work and sleep. You were on your best behavior at Kendra's, and I know we're safe here in SingleEarth, but I don't know where you draw your lines."

Fair enough.

"So the spell is to keep people from finding your homes?"

"More or less," Xeke answered. There was a lot more to

that "more or less," but Xeke's mind skipped over it, not forming the images clearly enough for Jay to pick them out. "So tell me: Should I be flattered you were looking for me, or nervous?"

Oh, right. He had a reason for wanting to find Xeke.

"I went into the woods, behind your apartment."

The words triggered *something* in Xeke, but again, Jay couldn't focus well enough to pick up on all of it. There was something about an arrangement. Politics, and a disgust of politics. Walking a tightrope.

"Did you have a nice walk?" Xeke asked.

"I found a woman, a shapeshifter, unconscious," Jay answered. "She still hasn't woken. We're not sure what's wrong with her. The doctors here think that maybe if—"

"You want to stop talking now," Xeke interrupted, with a spike of nervousness.

"Could you look at her, and let me know if—"

"I'm leaving."

"But—"

"Call me if you're interested in a night out on the town," Xeke said. "I'll leave my phone number at the front desk. But I'm not having this conversation with you." With that, he disappeared, too wary to even take the time to leave his number in person.

Jay scowled. He didn't like mysteries. He *really* didn't like it when people kept things from him.

He had never had an adolescent's panic over what other people were thinking, or whether they were thinking of him, or that sheer certainty that *everyone* was thinking about him all the time that most young teens had. No, from the start he had known when they lied; when they were pretending to be macho while scared; when it wasn't *quite* true when a mother said, "No, of course I'm not mad," when her young child accidentally broke an heirloom piece of china; and when people weren't thinking of him at all, even when they were in the middle of a conversation with him.

He understood. Everyone needed little lies to get them through the day, false courage to make them find real courage, and false comfort when something couldn't be repaired. Their minds were so complicated and their lives so intense that who could blame them that most of the time they weren't thinking about anything but themselves?

People were fascinating to Jay, but they weren't mysteries. That was why Xeke had fled. For some reason, he needed to be a mystery.

Jay could spend lazy hours as a cat basking in the sun, or as a lizard on a rock, or as a sparrow singing for the pure joy of the day. Others of his line used their empathy to become powerful healers of the body and mind, or to help them mediate conflict. Those who chose to go into human businesses made staggering amounts of money as psychotherapists, lawyers, marriage counselors, or industrial psychologists.

Jay had chosen the path of a hunter because whether he was a songbird or a kitten or a koi in a pool, there was one thing that could always pull him back: the challenge of a hunt.

He had been challenged, and like a bloodhound, he was now committed to this mystery. *Damn you, Xeke.*

CHAPTER 9

FIRST, HE HAD to get out of bed. He had recovered enough of his power that he could start focusing it on healing his wounds. Whatever foreign magic had kept Caryn from healing him while he was unconscious gave him no problems now.

He stood, and again sought the kitchen. He needed protein to make up for the power burned, and the blood lost.

Leftover fried chicken was a good start. He ate it cold, enjoying the grease, the crunch of the skin, and the softness of the meat beneath. He carried a leg bone with him as he walked through the parking lot to get a not-blood-covered shirt from the car. He also hoped he could find the directions he had used the night before.

Unfortunately, he would still have to backtrack all the way

to the highway, and then follow the directions the bloodbond had given him, in order to figure out where Kendra's Heathen Holiday had been—and from there, Xeke's apartment and the strange forest.

It was a reasonable plan.

First, he wrote the directions onto a piece of SingleEarth stationery and left that next to the unconscious shapeshifter, with a note saying, *This is near where I found her. Some kind of memory spell alters the ability to recall where it is. I will call if I find it again.*

He had to hold on to the doorjamb for a minute as a dizzy spell took him.

It was probably too soon to hunt, but he didn't need to fight anything yet. He could just go back to the party.

He would need to get dressed up again first, wouldn't he? Hmm.

Jeremy looked confused when Jay stepped in on him in the middle of his last intake for the day and asked, "Do you have an extra tuxedo I could borrow?"

"I'm a little busy, Jay." He had to finish up with this pa-tient, then change, pick up Caryn, and get to the much-dreaded gathering at his parents' house.

"So am I," Jay retorted. "And I need formal wear, quickly." He wanted to get there before midnight so he would be able to get a sense of how things were going and where he was, and then get out before the Devil's Hour. He couldn't afford to lose any more blood.

Jeremy apologized to his patient and pulled out his wallet.

He handed Jay a business card and said, "This is where we're getting our tuxes for the wedding."

Good enough. "Do you need the card back?"

"I have extras."

Great. Jay called as soon as he was back in the parking lot. Thankfully, Nikolas had forced him to be measured for the tux he had worn the first night at Kendra's gala, so he was able to give the store the exact size he needed. They had a few styles available for rental that evening and offered to have them ready for him to try on and choose from when he arrived at the store.

Wonderful service. No wonder Jeremy and Caryn were using them.

Within an hour, he had a tuxedo and was ready to return to a fabulous Christmas party filled with psychotic vampire artists who might or might not want to eat him come midnight.

The directions he had been given used landmarks instead of street names, and seemed to suggest going in circles. Nevertheless, Jay followed them to the letter, and once again traveled up the half-mile-long private driveway that led to Kendra's manor. Each window held a real flickering candle, and the trees out front sparkled with silver-blue lights. The front yard was decorated with elaborately carved white marble reindeer in various poses of grazing and leaping.

Before Jay passed through the entryway, he mentally reviewed his plan: walk in, get the lay of the land, establish clearly where he was, and *write that information down.* Meanwhile, he would try to find out why there was such a powerful spell on the area, and how great a range it covered. SingleEarth had some of the most powerful localized spells he knew of, but none of them approached the strength necessary to mess with his mind the way this one had.

As expected, Kendra's gala was still in full swing when he arrived shortly after ten. As much as he could without crashing his car, he had focused on his power and sense of magic along the way there, but he hadn't sensed anything that would indicate crossing the boundary of a spell.

Perhaps the spell itself wasn't around the town or the houses but around the *woods*? It might have bled out a bit to protect the houses closest to it.

If the spell didn't protect the vampires' dwelling areas specifically, then it might protect something hidden in that forest. He could check that out after he did some reconnaissance.

"Oh, you're back!" Brina exclaimed as soon as she saw him.

If he hadn't recognized the jewel tone of her mind, Jay never would have guessed that this was the same woman who had madly destroyed a series of paintings with her bare hands and nails an evening prior.

Dressed in an emerald-green gown with a plunging neckline and layers of soft skirts, Brina was resplendent. Her black hair shone, highlights reflecting all the colors around her, like a raven's feathers. It had been styled into an elaborate cascade of ringlets, pinned half up with mother-of-pearl combs and otherwise falling around her face and teasingly brushing the bare cream-colored skin of her shoulders.

Jay's mouth went dry, and for a moment every word and thought went out of his head.

She smiled and held out a hand gloved in white lace. He took it and kissed the back.

Her smile felt good, like sunshine.

He tried to remind himself that this woman was nuts, but part of that madness was a beautiful purity of thought. When she smiled, she emitted perfect joy. There was still sorrow like a quiet, deep pool in her mind, but she was determined to rise above it.

He wanted to pull her into his arms and hold her forever, protect her and cherish her and sculpt her and . . . These were not entirely his thoughts.

He didn't fight them, though. He had enough self-preservation not to sell himself into slavery or let her damage him, so he might as well enjoy her presence.

"I wish I knew how to dance," he said aloud. "If I did, I would ask you to join me."

"Sweetheart," she purred in response.

Don't forget why you're here, he reminded himself.

He debated broaching the subject of the shapeshifter with her, but something warned him off. Brina obviously didn't like focusing on anyone besides Brina.

He still wanted to dance with her.

"Brina, exactly the lady I was looking for."

The voice that cut between them was connected to a mind that instantly made Jay's proverbial hackles rise. There was something dark and calculating about it.

"Oh . . . you came," Brina answered, turning with a strong dash of irritation and a feigned smile.

The new vampire wasn't an artist, but there was something artistic about his spiderweb of a mind. Where Brina's mind put out waves of color and emotion, this one's mind was tightly woven, designed to be studied and approached, until Jay feared he would find himself ensnared.

Despite the distaste reverberating in her mind, Brina greeted the newcomer warmly, stepping forward to put herself into his embrace. He kissed her cheeks before moving back. "I have your portrait," she said. "It's in the gallery now. I do hope you don't need it until after the holiday is over? It's—one of my best works this year, and I would hate to take it off display so soon."

The other vampire heard as well as Jay did the telltale hitch in her voice as she described one of her "best works," but neither man challenged Brina on the untruth. Her best works had been destroyed by her own hands.

"Far be it from me to deprive you of such a joy," the other vampire replied.

Liar! Jay wanted to shout.

He drew back mentally and tried to put a face to the mind.

The vampire was dressed in a modern tuxedo. The shirt was a cream color that sat better against his burnt-sienna skin than classic white would have. His hair was long and dark, though it had been tied back out of the way.

He looked at Jay, his mind clinically analyzing him in a way that was cool, cautious, and utterly unconcerned as he noticed the aura of a witch and the smell of a recently oiled blade in a leather sheath, and instantly deduced, *Hunter*.

"And who is your companion?" the vampire asked Brina.

"Oh," Brina said. "This . . . Hmm, I'm not sure. But he's pretty, isn't he?"

"My lovely lady, it looks like you have a companion better suited to dancing than I am, so I will leave you to that," Jay half rambled, trying to take his leave of Brina gracefully, without attracting the further interest of this predator. Jay hadn't studied all the collected sketches and photographs of known vampires as much as some of his kin had, but he was pretty sure he was looking at one of Midnight's infamous trainers.

He knows what I am, Jay thought, forcing back the itch to try for a kill he knew was impossible. *He's prepared. Even if he were alone, it would be a long shot.* Many had tried, but in Midnight's entire history, there was no record of a hunter ever getting a knife into one of the trainers.

"Don't go!" Brina cried like a child at a tea party, grabbing Jay's wrist before he could take more than a step. Her sudden intensity was unsettling, and brought to mind Xeke's warning that this was not a woman who distinguished what or whom she did or didn't have a right to possess.

Jay gently but firmly extracted his wrist. "My apologies, Lady Brina, but I need to tear myself away from your company for a moment."

"Jay." Arms wrapped around him from behind as a familiar mind and body snuggled against him. "Dear Brina, you don't mind if I steal Jay for a while, do you?" Xeke crooned. "I'm sure he'll have time for you later, but you know how boys are."

Brina bit her lower lip, then said, "If you *insist.*"

Xeke looked at the trainer and nodded a cool greeting.

Something passed between the two men, something Jay almost wanted to analyze further, before he realized that Xeke felt he was protecting Jay from a double threat.

"Jay here is one of Kendra's guests," he said to the new vampire. "He was invited, with the full knowledge of his pedigree, and has behaved himself perfectly well. And now we're leaving."

With an arm firmly around Jay's waist, Xeke led him away, thinking furiously, *What kind of idiot are you, witch? Do you want to be her lapdog?*

"She can't—"

"*Witches* are freeblood," Xeke hissed, "as long as they violate none of Midnight's rules. *Hunters* are an entirely different matter, especially once they put themselves in our territory. You were invited here and weren't shy about what you were, so you're marginally safe, but if Jaguar had decided you were a threat to Brina, he could have handed you over to her in a heartbeat, and not a person in this house would have objected."

Why does he have so much power in Kendra's home? Jay wondered, just before Xeke swatted him upside the head, in a semi-playful yet very serious fashion that distracted him from pursuing the thought.

"What are you doing back here?" Xeke asked.

"Why shouldn't I be here?"

Xeke gave a long-suffering sigh before saying, "I don't think you came back to see me, and I hope you didn't come back to see Brina, which means you put in a great deal of effort to find a place that you're not supposed to find."

"Who is the woman from the woods?" Jay asked.

Xeke turned around and, in one smooth movement, slammed Jay up against the wall hard enough to knock his breath out, effectively distracting him from hearing Xeke's first-thought response.

"I don't know," Xeke answered honestly while Jay's eyes were still wide with surprise, "and I don't *want* to know. And you *shouldn't* want to know. If she's unconscious, maybe she's better off that way. If she wakes up and she wants you to know who she is, she'll tell you. So drop it, okay?"

"And if I won't?" Jay asked.

"Then I'm going to have to ask you to leave," Xeke said, words clear and precise, "and remind you that a hunter who trespasses on our land violates his freeblood privilege. I don't think you're crazy enough to risk that."

"Xeke," Jay said, "you have no idea how crazy I can be."

"You like risk. That's fine; I like to play games too," Xeke said with a brilliant smile. "Trust me when I say you don't want them to be real."

"You wouldn't keep me." Jay knew that for certain.

Xeke's response was chilling. "It wouldn't be up to me—this isn't my territory. You'd go to Kendra, or Jaguar, or probably Brina, given the sheer number of people who want to give her shiny baubles to keep her happy and placid. I don't have the clout to claim you as my own."

This time, Jay could find the thoughts related to Jaguar.

Midnight. Slave trade. Jaguar wasn't discussed much by hunters these days, but Xeke's caution made it clear that the trainer had regained at least some of the power and influence he had once had. That meant Midnight itself had become stronger than the hunters had begun to imagine.

"You're worried she belongs to someone," Jay said as he finally picked the thought—it should have been obvious, he realized—out of Xeke's mind. "You're worried the shapeshifter I found belongs to someone, and if you—" He broke off, because Xeke shook his head, still pinning Jay against the wall, and thinking, *He's so determined to hang himself, he doesn't even need rope.*

If the shapeshifter was an escaped slave, then anyone harboring or helping her had violated vampiric law and forfeited any freeblood privilege. If Xeke learned who she was, he and anyone allied with him could be claimed as payment unless Xeke turned the slave in. More important—to Jay, anyway—was the fact that since Jay was the one who had found her and taken her to SingleEarth, Midnight might decide he had stolen her.

But even that wasn't his biggest concern.

So far, Midnight was hiding, waiting in the wings . . . and gaining power. It hadn't had cause to challenge SingleEarth directly. No matter how badly Jay and other hunters would love to plant a knife in any of Midnight's trainers, no one wanted to start a fight that pitted the peaceful SingleEarth against that ancient evil.

Xeke thought at him, *You need to leave. Now.*

CHAPTER 10

JAY DIDN'T WANT to get himself sold into slavery over this. On the other hand, since the proponents of the slave trade were in Kendra's house for the party, they wouldn't be in the woods, would they?

And what did the vampires have to hide that was important enough and powerful enough that it was concealed with a spell that Jay couldn't even begin to discern?

Just one thing: Midnight.

The first version of Midnight's empire had been founded in the sixteen hundreds, around the time when Jay's line had come into existence. The vampires had effectively ruled the supernatural world through a combination of trade sanctions, economic incentives, and an iron threat to back up their laws.

Despite protections given to nonhumans, many of the witches were killed. The Light line was eradicated entirely, and the Arun and Vida lines, both of which were exclusively hunters, were cut down to a bare handful of survivors.

When the original Midnight had burned to the ground in 1804, there had been celebrations throughout the world. Unfortunately, though destroying its base of operations had weakened the empire sufficiently for other groups to regain control, the hunters at the time had not been able to eliminate the vampires themselves. Whispers of Midnight's return had become increasingly common lately.

The original Midnight had been out west, beyond the area claimed at that time by the newborn United States, in the no-man's-land where white men had not yet established dominion. Could the new one really have its heart *here*, arrogantly close not only to human civilization but to the headquarters of so many of Midnight's most serious enemies? Most of Jay's extended family, including almost all the vampire-hunting witches he knew, lived in New England. The Bruja guilds—a trio of mercenary groups that reputedly had originally been founded specifically to oppose Midnight—had their guild halls in Massachusetts and New York. Jay couldn't help but feel that such placement was meant to be a deliberate slap in the face.

If Midnight *was* here, Jay needed to know. If he was right, this would give hunters a chance to bring the empire to its knees before it could get back on its feet. He just needed information, and then he could contact his allies and begin to plan the hunt of a lifetime.

He changed clothes quickly in the backseat of his car and then went hiking behind Kendra's home, which bordered the same unnaturally quiet forest he had explored behind Xeke's apartment. Jay might not have been able to sense the magic directly, but the animals could.

Could the shapeshifter at SingleEarth have been damaged by this magic? She had an ominous forest in her mind, choking her mentally and keeping her a prisoner in her own brain. Could the menacing force Jay had sensed from her be Midnight?

He held his shields a little tighter. It would make it harder for him to sense magic, but he hadn't been able to do that yet anyway. He needed to make sure he was as protected as he could be.

He could feel the forest's heart. Most woods, especially older ones, had some sense of their center, but this was a young forest, easily impressionable; if it had a heart, it was probably one that had been thrust upon it magically, not one that had grown there organically.

Jay headed toward that pulse, keeping an eye—literally and magically—on the ebb and flow of the trees, underbrush, and snow. Magic's presence changed how natural things grew. The magic around this place might have been intended to hide something, so those who stumbled across it couldn't find their way back, but that power could also serve as a beacon.

And there it was—that high wrought-iron fence with the metal ravens at the top. Beyond, he could see stables and gardens. Following the fence brought him around to the front of the property, where a narrow road made a path like an arrow straight to the front door of a sprawling structure that seemed to be the spawn of a manor house and a medieval castle.

He sensed the guards at the front in time to avoid their notice, and stayed far enough away that he knew he wouldn't be seen from the road.

If Jay followed the road back, out of the forest, he would be able to determine where it intersected with a main road. He would know exactly where he was. He knew many hunters—some witches, some not—who would be interested in such information.

He kept parallel to the road from a safe distance away, trekking through the thick, snowy underbrush and checking back occasionally to make sure he was on course.

That was the theory, anyway, and it should have worked.

He had walked for about an hour, with the road always on his left, but suddenly he was facing the black gates of Midnight once again.

Impossible—except in the presence of a powerful spell, capable of disorienting him and rearranging his memories.

Time to pull out the big guns.

Jay Marinitch wasn't an average witch. In polite circles, he was considered a prodigy. Those less concerned with being polite referred to him as the idiot savant of his line. He had never met a power he couldn't match, and he wasn't about to start now.

He sat in the snow and drew his magic up around him. The Marinitch line's power was organic. He could read and speak to the trees and animals. He could feel the pulse and flow of natural power the way other people felt wind or water.

He focused his magic until he was able to feel every tree around him, and where he was in relation to every stone and every hibernating squirrel. He let himself flow into that power like a leaf on the wind, dissolving himself in it. If this other magic insisted on being invisible and subtly twisting his mind, he would give it no mind to focus on. He would make himself into nothing it could touch.

First, he explored. There were dozens of living people inside the building, and a couple of nonliving ones. The horses were happy, as was the large feline living inside . . . though she was restless as well.

Next, he touched the power that had been influencing him. It was hot and utterly nonnatural, and so not normally part of his own sphere of awareness. It twined into the land, twisting it.

He could prod his body into moving where he needed it to without really *belonging* to it, so he pushed it toward the boundary of the circle of power. He moved through the forest like the night, like shadow or a winter wind, without disturbing or being disturbed by the natural flow of energy through the forest.

He slid under the foreign power, around it, past it. He was a crafty little mouse, swift and agile but too small to be obtrusive.

Once finally outside the spell's radius, he sensed the difference like a pressure change. His ears popped as he returned fully to his body and stretched, reminding himself of the limiting confines of his flesh, bone, and muscle. He reminded himself of his human origin, and shook off the chill of the unnatural power in the forest that . . . that . . .

He leaned against the tree.

Midnight.

He had to hold on to that thought.

He knew what was inside the forest now.

But how was he going to get home?

First, he pressed a palm to one of the larger trees near the driveway to Midnight. The path itself was barely wide enough for two cars to pass, and was not marked in any way, so it was only by remembering the trees near it that he would later be able to recall where it was.

Since he didn't know where he was, there was no point in calling anyone to pick him up, so he started down the road in search of the nearest town.

Less than an hour later, he reached his goal. The town was dark and most of the stores were closed, but the old-fashioned stone monument in the town's center welcomed him to Pyridge, established 1612. The plaque beneath it spoke of a small town founded by a group that had suffered disagreements with their neighbors and so moved farther west. He wondered when this town, first built by rebels and malcontents, had been taken over by vampires.

CHAPTER 11

JEREMY AND CARYN pulled over to pick Jay up. They were both so tense that his head started to ache the instant he climbed into the car.

Their pre-wedding bickering didn't help.

"Stop that!" Caryn snapped when Jeremy sneezed as she followed Jay's circular directions back to Kendra's home.

"Sorry," Jeremy replied. "Something's going around school."

"I don't want you snotty and sneezing through your vows."

"I can't really help—"

"Let me," Jay said, deliberately interrupting. Leaning forward from the backseat, he touched fingertips to Jeremy's cheek.

"I thought witches can't heal illnesses," Jeremy remarked.

"It's more of an empathic thing than a healing thing," Jay explained.

Healing meant fixing something that was broken. When someone was sick, the body wasn't *broken*; symptoms were the result of the body doing what it needed to do to fight off an invader. Jay didn't have an incredible amount of practice dealing with diseases, but he could help boost the immune system and direct the body so it could fight off the common cold a little faster.

"You are so lucky that witches can't get sick," Jeremy said. "I have to worry about every cold that comes my way, while you two could share soda with a plague ward and be just fine."

"But it's so hard to find a good plague ward these days," Jay replied as he did the equivalent of some traffic-directing with Jeremy's body. "You should start to feel better in a few hours," he added, sitting back in his seat.

"Thanks."

"Do you want one of us to drive your car back to Single-Earth for you?" Caryn asked as she pulled into the driveway. "You feel wiped out."

He nodded tiredly. "Too much time fighting evil forests, I guess," he mumbled. Sensing her confusion, he added, "If someone else could drive, I'd appreciate that."

"No problem."

Jeremy was more than happy to drive Jay, so he could share his jitters as if the two men were old friends instead of mere acquaintances.

"How did Christmas dinner go?" Jay asked.

Jeremy shook his head. "As well as I could have expected," he answered. "Everyone behaved appropriately enough that we had to stay for the full dinner, even though everyone desperately wanted to leave."

It still seemed like a lot of stress to get a family's grudging blessing. Jay just didn't get weddings.

Then again, the closest Jay had come to a date in a long time was Xeke's inviting him out to a "night on the town." It was hard to find someone whose ego could hold up to a first date with someone who knew every random thought they had and had trouble following the out-loud conversation because the neurotic internal monologue was so much more interesting.

Could he bring Xeke as a date to the wedding?

Was he even invited to the wedding?

"Mind if I ask how you got stuck out here at this hour?" Jeremy asked.

"Investigating a spell," Jay answered, intentionally vague. There were times when it was best to keep things from others— like information that could get Jeremy stuck in the middle of an ownership feud with Midnight. SingleEarth regarded human members like Jeremy as equals, but to Midnight, they were pawns.

Deliberately returning the conversation to the one topic he knew would distract Jeremy from anything else, Jay asked, "Do you have a best man?"

Jeremy stared at him a bit longer than Jay was comfortable with, considering he was driving, before answering, "Yes. Though I was wondering if you would be willing to be an usher? Caryn suggested that that empathy of yours might help you keep the guests from coming to blows."

"I can do that," he answered. Could be fun.

First, though, he needed to settle the mystery of this shapeshifter once and for all. It would be a damn shame if the wedding were spoiled by eminent war with Midnight over a comatose shapeshifter.

Once back at SingleEarth, Jay changed into dry clothes, picked up a few of the kinds of trinkets he usually made fun of Vireo for using, and then went back to the shapeshifter's room.

This time he would be more careful, better armed and armored. He would find her mind, and he would bring her high enough to the surface to determine what they needed to do with her.

Maybe she wasn't a slave, but a visitor or an employee of Midnight. Or maybe she had gone into the woods, become lost in the spell that had tried to trap Jay, and been unable to break free.

The first step Jay took was to write a note and pin it to the door, saying, *Complex magic. Do not disturb.* Thinking again, he revised it: *Do not disturb except in case of unexplained life-threatening injuries.* It would suck if the healers let him die because he left a badly worded note.

He adjusted the position of the shapeshifter's bed so he could form a circle around her. He marked the perimeter with a combination of hematite, agate, and obsidian stones, some tumbled and some rough. All of them had been created through volcanic activity and still held the power of that heat boiling up through the surface of the earth. The magic in Jay's blood also came from fire—from the elemental Leona, who had bonded herself to his kind thousands of years ago—so the stones would simultaneously boost his power and help ground him. The hematite—a silver-gray iron ore—would act as a tether so he wouldn't get trapped in the shapeshifter's mental and magical woods again. One of the obsidian pieces he had chosen had been flaked into an arrowhead; its edge was as sharp as a razor and cut through his skin easily as he drew it across the fingertips of his right hand.

He touched each stone in his circle, linking his blood to the ancient volcanic power and the solidity of rock. The world seemed to hold its breath as he touched the last, sealing the circle around himself and the silent shapeshifter.

Another power wailed in fury.

There was magic inside her that did not like the fire one bit.

Jay stepped forward into her mental hell.

What do you want? the forest snarled at him. The trees nearby twisted, writhing in irritation. *How can we help her if you keep intruding?*

The forest ransacked his mind. It found his fear of Midnight, his fear that the vampire's empire might threaten his kin, and his anger that it had once nearly destroyed them. It found his plan to share Midnight's location with other hunters. It found his conviction that Midnight *must* be cut down again, and forever.

It knew that he could speak to the trees and had merged

with them in order to slip away from the circle of magic that had tried to trap him in Midnight's forest.

It knew how much he despised being trapped.

The more this power learned about him, the more welcoming it became.

We can't reach her, it lamented. *They locked her away from us.*

The images that came with the words were brutal.

The shapeshifter was a slave. One of the trainers had claimed her hundreds of years ago and had worked tirelessly to break her mind and turn her into the perfect . . . Pet. That was the name the trainer had given her.

Until him, she had been nameless, a priestess dedicated to her people, her land, and her power. She had been holy; he had made her profane. She had been . . .

She had been beaten, and broken, and with each stroke she had built stronger walls inside her mind as she had tried to protect something so precious that it alone could *never* be sacrificed to the trainer.

Me, the power whispered. *My child let herself be savaged so she could protect me. She sealed herself off from me, and now I cannot even tell her that it is safe to return.*

Is it worth saving her, if Midnight then comes to claim her? Jay wondered.

The other power responded as if Jay had spoken aloud. *If you can reach her, and help me reach her, then she will be all I need to destroy those who hurt her.*

"You mean Midnight? The trainers?" Jay asked. "She could fight them?"

You will not need to fear them anymore.

"I'll try to reach her," Jay said. "I'm not sure if I can, but I'll try."

There are many traps in her mind. I will do my best to protect you.

First, he needed to be something fast and powerful, to get through the brambles. A stag would have been nice, but Jay had never had the opportunity to study one well enough to know its thought patterns. A lynx would be too small. Wolf?

Here.

The thought came along with the overwhelming sense of . . . *not* a house cat. Not a lynx or a bobcat. Bigger. Mountain lion.

That would work.

Jay stretched his new body and felt the forest respond with wary interest. This form was known to it. Was the shapeshifter a cougar?

He fought his way through the forest, his lithe body wriggling out of the way when branches tried to form a cage, and his thick fur shrugging off even the worst of the brambles.

As he reached Midnight's black iron fence, crows and ravens began to dive-bomb, shrieking. He batted them out of the sky, his jaws sending feathers and avian blood splattering as he made his way inexorably closer.

He changed shape only momentarily, and a much smaller cat slipped easily between the black iron bars, before the mountain lion was running across the open front yard.

He struck the front door with claws extended. The building itself began to bleed and writhe.

Where are you? he called.

She was in there, somewhere.

Acting on instinct, he shredded the door, and the walls next to it. They looked like hardwood and stone, but they tore like flesh. Once he had cut a hole, he padded through it into a quiet, shadowed grove of white birch trees.

In the middle lay a woman, her body bleeding from a thousand cuts, her black flesh burned and slashed, her hair matted, and her moss-green eyes wide with fear.

"No!" she shouted. "You can't be here! No one can be here!"

"I'm here to help you," Jay said.

Started to say. Or roar. He wasn't sure how far he made it before the ground shook, knocking him off his paws. The trees wept. Whatever power had spoken to him earlier had followed him here.

"Is she—"

Before he could finish speaking, he was thrown brutally backward, into his own flesh in the shapeshifter's room.

He was alone. Her bed was empty, and the door was standing open.

Nothing should have been able to get in or out of the circle he had built, but as he looked around, he realized that several of the stones on one side had fractured before being pushed aside.

What on earth had he just released?

CHAPTER 12

WHATEVER HAD JUST spoken to him in the shape-shifter's mind, then thrown him out and fractured his circle, had left him so fried that he kept spacing out as he attempted to gather his tools back into their bag. At one point, he jumped when he spaced out for a moment and suddenly found Jeremy standing in front of him, holding a large book titled *Ancient Elavie Cultures*. The human was looking from the note on the door, to Jay, to the empty bed.

"It's okay to come in now," Jay said, trying to focus on the human's mind but unable to glean anything more than static.

"Did you magic her away somewhere?" Jeremy asked.

"I woke her up, and the next thing I knew, she was gone."

He wasn't ready to go into further details, such as promises to destroy Midnight. Maybe he should have asked a little more about that—like *How?* or *When?*

Instead, he asked Jeremy, "Are you still awake, or already awake?"

"A combination of the two," Jeremy admitted. "Having trouble sleeping. Nerves. I thought I'd try to solve our mystery, but I guess it's a moot point now."

"What's the book?" he asked Jeremy. *Elavie* was Single-Earth's scientific term for shapeshifters.

Jeremy plopped down to sit on the floor next to Jay.

"The way her power reacted to yours made me think about the way some of the older Elavie, especially the ones from cultures with additional magic, can live hundreds of years or more. When I started looking at the older cultures, I found a reference to the Shantel."

"You're on the right track with the age thing. Who are the Shantel?"

"I found them in a book about language, actually. Many of the older shapeshifter cultures make reference to something or someone called a *sakkri*. The serpiente use the word now to describe a kind of dance, but their myths say that dance is the remnant of an ancient magical ritual. The Mistari use it to mean something said or done to mislead. And the Shantel used the term to refer to the magic that kept them protected, and to the witch who controlled that power."

Jeremy paused with a self-satisfied smile, obviously finding that little fact interesting enough that it took him a moment to realize he hadn't yet answered Jay's question.

"Right," he said, continuing on. He flipped pages as he spoke. "It took me a while to find anything more about the Shantel, since they were incredibly isolationist, and seem to have entirely disappeared in the last couple centuries. They were shapeshifters—leopards and mountain lions—and were considered one of the great magical powers of the last millennium, up there with the shm'Ahnmik and the Azteka."

Both of the other cultures Jeremy referenced were mostly gone. There were pockets of Azteka left, but none of their famous bloodwitches, and some believed that the entire falcon civilization—known as the shm'Ahnmik—might have been no more than part of serpiente myth, like the humans' Atlantis.

"You think the shapeshifter I found was some kind of Shantel witch?"

"The Shantel describe their spirit-witch as white and silver in her leopard form, but ink-black in human form, with white markings to make her power clear to all who see her. Sound familiar?"

The description fit, including the fact that Jay had been given a cougar form with which to seek her.

"She didn't have a name," Jay said, recalling that fact from his sojourn within her power. "There was something about her remaining nameless, to—"

"Yes!" Jeremy interrupted, flipping to another page. "It says here the Shantel believed that 'only by remaining nameless and unclaimed by family or lover could the *sakkri* commune with and command the immortal powers of nature.' I don't have a clue what that means, but any magic-user put in a group with falcons and Azteka has to be scary powerful."

"I *think* she's on our side," Jay answered uneasily. At least, he *hoped* she was. The fact that she had disappeared without speaking to anyone didn't bode well.

"The Shantel were never warlike," Jeremy continued, still looking down at his book. "Even during Midnight's reign, they just used their magic to keep their people safe. They never fought back. They're one of the only shapeshifter cultures we know of that no one ever went to war with." He looked up at the bed. "Did she say where she was going?"

"She didn't say anything," Jay answered.

If she came from such a peaceful culture, Jay didn't know what she expected to do against Midnight. On the other hand, two centuries in slavery was bound to change a person.

"Jeremy, you didn't happen to find anyone else who might know about the Shantel, did you?" Jay asked, trying to keep the words casual.

"I've been trying to see if any of the older vampires in SingleEarth might know something," he said, "but I know the humans and witches here better. Vampires don't often come in for medical attention, you know?"

Who did Jay know who was old enough to have survived Midnight but wasn't allied or otherwise tied to Midnight? The list was pretty short. Even vampires who disapproved of the slave trade tended to try not to cross the empire. Nikolas and Kristopher, Sarah's friends, were fifty years too young—and Jay wasn't certain he wanted to get them involved, anyway. He definitely didn't want to get *Sarah* involved, not with Midnight, not when she was still trying to find her place in the vampiric world.

Wait.

There was a group Jay knew, and SingleEarth knew, that rumor claimed had been founded to fight Midnight. Few of their members were vampires, unsurprisingly, but some were shapeshifters or Tristes old enough to remember those days.

The Bruja guilds were technically three groups, known as Crimson, Onyx, and Frost. They had been founded during Midnight's reign in opposition to the slave-holding vampires, and many of their members still considered themselves vampire hunters, though in recent years they had branched out into other illegal and semi-legal actions.

Frost and SingleEarth had recently managed to find a mutually beneficial and profitable arrangement. Frost provided bodyguarding and other protective services, as well as a strong arm to help SingleEarth with the increasingly complicated process of securing mostly legal documents for individuals whose lifestyles or life spans made anything requiring a birth certificate or social security card difficult.

Jay went to the main SingleEarth office to find the contact information for their Frost liaison. He had to sweet-talk the secretary to convince her to give him the information without reporting the request, but he was soon back in his room and on his cell phone, hoping he would be able to reach someone quickly.

He realized he had walked out on Jeremy without a word

of explanation or apology. Jeremy probably wouldn't take it personally.

A voice answered the phone, "Lydia's Candy Shop, please hold."

Was there was some kind of code he was supposed to give? For all he knew he had dialed a wrong number and this actually *was* a candy shop.

Maybe he should go back to the secretary and check on how to handle this, or even go through official channels. Better safe than sorry? But which was safer—going through official channels and possibly dragging SingleEarth into the mess he might have made, or trying to do this on his own so at the worst he was the only one likely to end up sold into slavery?

By the time someone came back on the line, Jay had decided it didn't hurt to try.

"Thank you for holding. How can I help you?"

"This is Jay Marinitch. I'm calling from SingleEarth, and I—"

"Is this the best number to reach you?" the voice asked, interrupting.

"Um . . . yes," he replied. "It's my cell phone."

"I'll have someone call you back."

The line went dead.

It could still be a rude candy shop, but the likelihood he had reached Frost was high. Jay left his room and scavenged the kitchen while he waited. The breakfast pickings were pretty slim. He picked up a stale donut, and then his phone rang.

"Hello?"

"Jay Marinitch?"

"Yes?"

Candy or mercenaries?

"I was told you called. What can I do for you?"

This was why he hated phones. "May I ask who's calling?" he asked.

The voice on the other side of the line laughed and said, "No. *You* called *us*. What do you need?"

Not a candy shop. He might still make an ass of himself, but at this point, who could blame him?

"I need some information," he said, "or a contact who can get me that information. Someone familiar with a culture that went extinct around the fall of Midnight but who isn't *allied* with Midnight."

A slight pause from the other side of the line—man or woman? Jay couldn't tell.

"What culture?"

"The Shantel. I want to know about their magic, and their spirit-witch, the . . . *sakkri*."

"Aah." A short pause, and then, "I'll call you back."

The phone beeped, and the screen announced, *Call Lost*.

Weird.

Jay wasn't used to cloak-and-dagger, at least in the meta-phorical sense. Cover businesses and cryptic, androgynous phone voices made him antsy.

He wanted to *hunt*, the way a cheetah hunts, just for the pure joy of tearing into something and bringing it down. He *needed* to take on Midnight; it was a cancer in the free world, run by vicious, evil creatures who didn't hesitate to violate any natural law in their quest for domination. But that hunt required careful planning, and coordination with other hunters. *Caution. Patience.* And now, *wandering,* waiting for someone else to give him information.

The winter morning was crisp and freeze-the-bones cold, so even with his heavy jacket on Jay had to use a thread of power to keep himself from shivering.

You all right?

The faint mental touch from Lynx made him smile. *Restless,* he answered, *but not hurt. Where are you?*

Not far. Lynx liked Haven #2. There were just enough big-predator shapeshifters for their scents to scare away coyotes, the only local predator that could be a danger to him. Also, Caryn knew Lynx, and always kept a stash of turkey jerky on hand. *Do you need me?*

I'm okay, Jay answered, just as his phone started vibrating. It was the same voice as before.

"If you're sure you want to meet with her, I can set you up with someone who specializes in archaic magic. But I'll warn you, she might eat you alive."

"Literally or figuratively?"

"That depends on whether or not she likes you."

"Fantastic. How do I set up the meeting?"

The individual on the other side of the line took information about Jay's location and means of transportation, then gave him an address and the instruction to, "leave within the hour if you don't want to be late." Then the caller hung up, without saying whether Jay was looking for a short balding woman with a rose between her teeth or a giant ferret.

Going hunting? Lynx asked in response to Jay's increased excitement.

Going talking first, he replied. *But hopefully we'll hunt soon.*

CHAPTER 13

JAY COULDN'T BEGIN to recall where he had left his gloves, though he wished he did when he set his hands to the steering wheel. He half expected his GPS to swear at him for waking it up when it was so cold.

He programmed in the address from the mysterious telephone voice and let out a whine when he realized it was almost three hours away. He wouldn't get there until noon, *if* he didn't hit traffic.

After an hour on the highway, he turned on to progressively smaller, more winding roads. Midday became early afternoon, and he hadn't yet arrived, because he had needed to drop his speed to avoid spinning out on the increasingly common patches of black ice on the badly plowed, poorly marked back roads.

Whoever he was visiting, she didn't like visitors. Jay missed the unmarked driveway the first time and had to turn around. His tires got a beating as he bumped his way across potholes big enough to bury a body in.

Finally he reached the house, which was overhung by several bare maple trees.

I hope this is the right place, Jay thought as he walked up the narrow, recently shoveled path. There didn't seem to be a bell, so he knocked on the door.

The person who answered the door was a young woman, maybe twenty years old at most, whose brown eyes had dark circles beneath them. She exuded no particular thoughts but a sense of bone-deep weariness that made Jay want to curl up and sleep for a month just looking at her.

"Are you the person I'm supposed to meet?" he asked.

She stared at him for long, silent moments before saying, "I doubt it. Rikai's in her study. I think she's expecting someone."

Rikai!

The phone caller's warning made sense now; like vampires, Tristes needed to feed, but they did so by absorbing raw power instead of by taking blood. Of the three Wild Cards, Jay had been excited to meet Xeke but hadn't ever wanted to meet Rikai.

Nervously, Jay followed his guide to the study.

The walls in the hallway were painted a cool gray-rose color above wood paneling that had been stained silvery birch. The floor was carpeted in a two-tone beige. The overall effect was stylish but not *warm.*

Rikai's study was lit by only two candles—a fat pillar on top of the fireplace mantel, and a beeswax taper on a short table near the door. They barely illuminated the full wall of glass-front bookcases, a desk scattered with unidentifiable objects, and two chairs that were somehow ominous. Maybe Jay was simply crediting the atmosphere to the chairs, but he didn't want to sit down.

It took a moment for him to realize Rikai was even in the room, partially because her long black hair matched a body sheathed from neck to ankle to wrist in more black, but more so because his mind registered *nothing*.

Jay had occasionally met people who could put up walls against him, or who tried to fight his power. He had rarely met an individual who was a complete blank.

"Jay Marinitch," she said. Her voice had a soft lilt, lower than he might have expected, like the sound of ocean waves moving over sand. "Of the Marinitch witches. Please, sit."

Jay looked to the chair nearest him, and hesitated.

"The power you're sensing isn't intended for you," Rikai said. "If you can't bring yourself to overcome your instincts enough to sit in a chair to speak to me, you might as well leave now."

Jay sat, even though doing so made his skin crawl. The chair was nice enough, but whatever power Rikai had going on here made his teeth ache.

Rikai leaned back in her deep, plush chair, stretching her legs out in front of her and propping her feet on some kind of twisted sculpture that apparently doubled as a footrest. Her dark eyes had a strange shine to them as she looked at Jay.

"So. Why do you want to know about the Shantel?"

"Do I need a reason?" he asked. He wasn't coy by nature, but he hadn't expected to be asked *why* by a contact set up through Bruja.

"You're a witch, an empath, and a hunter. You are not a scholar. You *are* tainted by all sorts of interesting power, though."

"Such as?"

"Answer my question, and maybe I'll answer yours."

She leaned forward, bending at the waist, reminding him of a praying mantis. He had a powerful feeling that it would be unwise to lie to her.

"I think I've met a Shantel," he answered. "Specifically, a *sakkri*. I'd like to know more about her abilities."

"Out of pure idle curiosity, oh?" Rikai replied. "How very SingleEarth, but utterly unlikely for *you*. Where did you stumble across the spirit-witch of a dead civilization?"

Cautiously, he said, "Answering that question may put you at risk, which I would rather not do."

"Sweet of you." Did she ever say anything sincere? "If something you say to me here travels beyond my home to cause me problems, it will be because *you* carried it with you. That said, share, and I'll judge whether it's worth letting you out of here alive. If it comforts you, I rarely find information threatening."

Nope. That didn't comfort him.

"I suspect she used to be a slave in Midnight," he explained. "I believe she was taken into Midnight before the fall of the first empire, and somehow remained—"

"Oh," Rikai interrupted. "Pet."

Jay stiffened. That was what the shapeshifter remembered the trainer calling her. He had been the only one with the audacity to name the *sakkri*. "You know her?"

"Before they were shapeshifters, the Shantel were a Native American tribe whose magic came from their connection to an earth elemental. After Leona claimed them, the combined powers made them strong enough that even Midnight was never able to fully control them. At any given time, the Shantel had dozens of trained witches, but their true strength was wielded through their *sakkri,* a priestess whose only function was to communicate with and command the earth elemental who had first given them magic.

"But Pet is . . . well, nothing, anymore. Midnight's trainers did their jobs well. That woman hasn't had a spark of free will in her for more than two hundred years, and since her power requires that she be neither owned nor named, it's impossible for any would-be master to use her power for his own purposes. Last I heard, she belonged to Daryl."

"What if she was fixed somehow? Healed?" Jay asked. "What would she be capable of?"

He wanted to ask outright, *Could she really bring down Midnight?* But he didn't dare breathe those words aloud. Rikai wasn't allied with Midnight, but Jay wasn't sure how she felt about the empire, either.

Rikai scoffed at his question. "Anyone who has ever tried will tell you it can't be done."

"Hypothetically," Jay said. "What would she be capable of?"

"Even if through some miracle Pet were restored to her former state, the *sakkri* was always forbidden from violence or bloodshed. I doubt she would even know how to fight. She might be able to hide herself or others from those who choose to pursue her as escaped property, but I'm not even sure she could still do that. Elementals gain power through the mortals bound to them, often as they are worshipped. The Shantel have been gone for centuries. Their elemental would have weakened."

"I think the Shantel elemental spoke to me, through Pet," Jay said.

"It *spoke* to you?" Rikai asked, sounding intrigued. "You're lucky you're still alive. I suppose using Pet as a conduit protected you. What did it say?"

Moment of truth?

Not yet. "I'd rather not share. But it didn't seem weak."

"A weak elemental is still the strongest thing you will ever encounter in your life, short of a stronger elemental or a bona fide god, should such a thing exist," Rikai answered. "Even now, the power it left on you from your brief encounter is dripping off you in buckets."

"*What?*" Now he knew how people felt when they spoke to him. What was she talking about? "Is that a good thing or a bad thing?"

"It's the only reason you and your 'rather not share' are still sitting in my study," Rikai answered with a smile that was more predatory than pleasant. "You have traces of half a dozen different magics on you, which I suspect you gained by wandering into areas where you were not welcome. For Xeke's sake, I'll warn you that some of those spells learn. Escaping them will prove more difficult next time."

"Thanks," he whispered. It had been hard enough to escape them last time. "Xeke mentioned me?"

"No."

Then how . . . No, never mind. "Do elementals, I don't know, grandstand? This one offered a lot, but you're saying it probably can't deliver."

Rikai laughed. "Little witch, most elementals think of themselves as *gods*. They crave worship, and I have never met one capable of admitting to its own limitations. Most of them will offer anything, in exchange for a mortal's devotion. Grandstanding, as you put it, is all they do."

So the Shantel elemental probably couldn't do anything. It hadn't been strong enough to reach its *sakkri* on its own, but it had obviously been desperate to do so. It knew Jay was afraid of Midnight, so it had told him what he wanted to hear.

Simultaneously disappointed and relieved, Jay rose to his feet, saying, "Thank you for your time. You've been very helpful."

Rikai didn't bother to stand. "I had thought your question might be more interesting."

"I'm kind of glad it wasn't," he answered.

Jay couldn't help the shapeshifter unless she asked for his help. In the meantime, if the *sakkri* went up against Midnight and failed, it would be sad, but if Jay understood Midnight's rules right, the mess wouldn't land on SingleEarth. The *sakkri's* so-called owner would be the one held responsible.

Honestly, if he awoke after two centuries of slavery to discover his entire culture had been destroyed, Jay would probably be willing to throw away his life on a hopeless quest for vengeance, too. What did she have to lose?

CHAPTER 14

MIND ONLY SLIGHTLY more at ease, Jay followed Rikai's servant to the doorway and then tackled the long drive back to SingleEarth. He ordered his usher tux for Jeremy and Caryn's wedding, but when he found the bride and groom fussing over a seating chart—*No, we can't place Aunt Celia so close to Mark; she's an uncontrolled psychic and won't be able to screen out his schizophrenia*—he fled to the library.

I'll update them later.

He tried searching for more information about the Shantel, but the quiet library with its large plush chairs suggested another plan.

In his head, though, voices were arguing. All he wanted was

to drift peacefully, but he couldn't quiet the furious, faceless entities whose voices intruded on his dreamworld.

Do you have no control over your children? They are vicious, hungry creatures without any compassion or drive except to destroy and enslave.

Unlike some of our kind, I know the difference between an immortal and a god. If there is a deity greater than us, then surely he is the one who gave mortals free will. Whine to him, not me.

You stole my priestess!

If I had not stolen your priestess, she would have been dirt long ago, just like all the others.

We trusted you.

That was foolish.

"I want to see the pretty witch!"

Brina's voice, apparently still musical even at high volumes, pulled Jay out of bizarre dreams that left him groggy and disoriented. When in the last few days had he had any real sleep? He kept trying, but he had barely catnapped. Now deep night was pressing against the library windows.

Brina had probably woken at sunset.

The pretty witch. Jay was pretty sure that meant him. He briefly debated the merits and downsides of presenting himself, versus hiding behind a bookcase.

Other voices scrambled to reply to Brina, but Jay couldn't make out the words. He could feel their anxiety, though, and their knowledge that things might get messy before someone trained to handle this kind of situation showed up.

The problem was that Jay *was* one of the people they were waiting for. As a hunter living at SingleEarth, he was expected to deal with threats like this.

He smoothed his hair back in its ponytail—Brina was not one to respond well to individuals presenting themselves to her unkempt—then followed the shouting.

The vampiric mediator at Haven #2 was a fledgling of Mira's line. As Jay approached, Brina picked the young vampire up bodily and threw her down the hall hard enough to splinter the wall. Brina had just turned to Vireo, who had ducked his head into the hall to see what was going on, when Jay said, "Lady Brina. So good to see you. How can I help you?"

To Vireo, he thought as clearly as possible, *I've got this. Stay out of the way, and keep bystanders away.*

Vireo had the authority to kick him out of a sickroom, but this was Jay's field.

"Little witch, I am very cross with you," Brina said with a pout.

"I am sorry I had to leave earlier," Jay replied, keeping his tone as absolutely sincere and sycophantic as he could. Brina liked flattery. She expected it, and it calmed her. "I hope you found a more worthy dance partner than I."

Brina almost looked mollified, for a moment, before she frowned and snapped, "You have no idea why I'm upset."

"Then I apologize once again," he said, creeping a bit closer but not yet drawing his knife.

It probably wouldn't be a good idea to kill Brina in Single-Earth territory. Her allies included some of the most powerful vampires.

What was bothering her? Jay still wasn't at his best, and Brina was a madwoman on a rampage, her thoughts fragmented and angry. She genuinely believed he *should* know why she was angry, but that was all he could pick up.

"Fair lady, what can I do for you?" he asked.

"My maid has gone missing."

The words evoked a sense of fear and loss, which hit Jay low in the gut. Daryl had given her this particular servant, long ago, and Brina was totally unable to manage her household without . . .

Oh . . . crap.

Rikai had said that the Shantel spirit-witch had belonged to Daryl. Of course he had given that powerful, valuable slave to his much loved sister, possibly bequeathed upon his death.

Putting the bits and pieces of previous memories together with her current thoughts, Jay could almost see how it had played out. Those moss-green eyes spotting her mistress swinging from the rafter. Cutting her down and trying to calm her.

Only to have Brina throw her out of the house for her audacity.

And then Jay had picked her up and walked away with her.

Now Brina was here, demanding Jay. Xeke had tried to warn Jay not to ask about the woman he had found. Jay had been talking to him in the middle of a room full of individuals with vampiric hearing and alliances to Midnight. Any of them could have heard what little he had said to Xeke.

Stupid, stupid, stupid.

"If you'll simply turn her over," Brina said, "we can go our separate ways peacefully."

That was going to be a problem.

"And if I cannot do that?" Jay asked carefully.

"I will allow you to replace her with something of equal value."

Brina's voice was cool, but Jay could feel fury under the surface. Jay stole Pet. He needed to make it right.

"May I ask her value?"

"Pet reads and writes twelve languages," Brina replied, "and has served in my household for two hundred years. She knows my schedule, and all my contacts and preferences. She knows the proper storage and usage of all my painting supplies, and is not negatively affected by fumes from the oils . . . unlike my previous housemaid, whose eyes started bleeding. So tell me, how much do *you* think she's worth?"

She wasn't actually looking for a number.

"I am sorry that your maid has gone missing," he said, not about to freely *admit* to walking off with her invaluable so-called possession. "If I see her, I will—"

"You *have* her," she said. "I know you do. You came to the party to tell me you had her, but Exequías distracted you. Give her back."

She considered the things she needed to deal with now that

her head slave was missing, such as buying and distributing food for the other help, or procuring medical supplies. With the shapeshifter absent, such activities were simply not getting done.

It was a temporary measure—Jay would make it a temporary measure with a knife if he had to—but he said, "Perhaps I can assist you until she is returned." He didn't want to make this a SingleEarth problem. If the powers that be in Midnight decided he had stolen the slave, he could be claimed as payment. He would not ask SingleEarth to harbor him. "I just need to tell someone where I am headed, so they don't think you've stolen me away," he said.

Brina nodded.

Jay stepped into the front office, with Brina just behind him.

"There has been some confusion as to the location of some of Lady Brina's property," he explained to the nervous-looking secretary, who had overheard the entire conversation. "I'm going to go with her for now to help with her household until this is sorted out. Would you make sure Caryn is notified?"

Caryn and the rest of their kin would be able to retrieve him if necessary, or otherwise smooth the way for him to escape. As a last resort, he had his knife.

In the meantime, he was hardier than a human; oil paints wouldn't harm him, and he could make sure Brina didn't accidentally starve her staff.

"You may drive," Brina said. "I did not bring a vehicle. I will give you directions."

So kind of her.

He drove; she directed. He noticed they were going into Pyridge just in time to feel them cross the border of the circle into Midnight's land.

Why *did* he feel it this time? What had changed?

They stopped in front of a Victorian-style home with large bay windows. He parked in the driveway, and Brina "allowed" him to open her door and escort her onto the porch.

The house was pretty, he decided. It would have been odd for a vampire to have so many windows, but sun wasn't actively dangerous to vampires—only fatiguing—and Brina was an artist. She needed the light.

Brina opened the front door without a key, and a lanky feline launched itself at her.

She caught the spotted beast in her arms and pulled it to her chest with no concern for the white and gold fur that stuck to the silk bodice of her dress. The cat looked up at Jay with pale blue eyes and then looked away, apparently unconcerned.

He reached for it mentally, and received a sense of *New toy? Not in the mood to play now. Dinner? It's time for dinner. Dinner!*

The cat nipped at Brina's cheek, demanding food. It wasn't starving, but whatever routine its meals had been set to had been disrupted, and it was annoyed that Brina seemed to want to snuggle instead of feeding it *right now!*

"I think your cat is hungry," Jay said.

Food! it demanded with a plaintive yowl.

I'm working on it! he replied. The cat's ears twitched and its tail lashed, as if to say, *I did not give you permission to speak to me.*

"Oh," Brina said, dropping the cat. "Well, you can feed it. The kitchen is somewhere around here. I need . . . to get back to my work."

She disappeared, leaving Jay alone in the front hall with a cross cat staring at him with ice-blue eyes.

CHAPTER 15

JAY TESTED THE front door. It had no apparent lock but didn't budge at a casual push.

Well, then. He would deal with that later, after SingleEarth had some time to work out this snarl, and Jay had made an attempt to reason with Brina. For now, he had more important things to do.

The cat's body was dense and its ears rounded, as if it had some wildcat in it. Hopefully that would be useful; his connection with Lynx made it easier for him to communicate with other felines.

Where's the food? Jay asked it.

It darted from the room. *Follow!*

Funny—the cat and Brina seemed to have a lot in common.

Jay scraped a can of food into a hand-painted porcelain cat bowl, then watched while the irate feline ate. Once it had finished its meal, he wrestled with it for a few minutes, gradually getting himself more attuned to its mind and letting it investigate his. The cat didn't have a sense of what a witch was, and didn't care, but it was willing to tolerate his catness as long as he maintained proper deference.

When Jay inquired what the household was like, he received a mixed bundle of images.

The person who normally gave it food was also somewhat feline. The cat had tried to talk to her, but Pet's cat wasn't allowed to talk back. She was only allowed to act human, feed the cat, and order the other slaves to clean up and provide playtime.

There was one slave who normally provided the most playtime, but the cat had not seen him in a while, since the food-giving slave with a cat hidden inside had disappeared.

The cat thought of Brina as two people. One was a love giver. One was evil. The cat could normally tell quickly which was which, and when *that* Brina was around, the cat ran outside.

Outside? Jay asked, wondering if there was another exit.

The cat showed him to its cat door, installed in place of one of the panes of a downstairs window. It was too small for a person, but Lynx might be able to fit through if he came looking for Jay.

Do you know where the playtime slave is? Jay asked.

Upstairs, the cat replied, showing him to a grand staircase. At the top of the stairs was a landing, and then a locked door.

Key? Jay asked, trying the doorknob. He was pretty sure the lock here was mundane, not mystical.

The cat didn't understand the concept of a key, only of doors opening or closing.

Who normally opens the door?

Images of Brina and Pet answered him.

If I were a key, where would I be? Jay wondered, making the cat twitch its ears.

First you're a cat, and now you want to be this key thing?

He had learned from past experience that trying to explain a figure of speech to a cat was a lost cause, so instead he proposed, *I have a hunting game. If we succeed, I think we may be able to find the playtime slave. There is an object that the food slave would have used whenever she opened the door.*

Cat did not help much in the search, instead spending most of the time pouncing at Jay, putting occasional teeth marks in his pants.

Beyond a well-stocked kitchen and dining room, there was a parlor with elegant furniture the cat shied away from. It evoked memories of severe reactions from the master of the house—Lord Daryl, Jay believed. He tried to explain to Cat that Daryl was dead, and received a haughty response that could best be translated as *Duh.*

He tried to clarify that Daryl was dead in a way that meant he wouldn't be walking around anymore, as opposed to dead in the way of a vampire, but the cat bit him hard on the leg to close the subject and then decided to fix the problem by climbing the stairs, standing up with its front paws against the door, and yowling, screaming, at the top of its lungs, *Open this door!*

We need the key, Jay tried to explain.

What is this key thing you're obsessed about? it snapped back. *Leave the key. I don't care about the key. Tell them to open the door! They don't listen to me.*

Tell them to open the door? Jay asked, feeling more than a little stupid.

Yes! the cat said, adding an angry hiss.

Jay climbed the stairs once more and knocked on the slick wooden door. At first, he received no response, which in some ways made him feel better. Maybe the door did open on this side, and he hadn't been incredibly stupid. At the cat's demands, he tried a second time, and was rewarded by rustling on the other side, followed by the *snick* of a lock being turned, followed by . . .

Need.

His eyes saw a human being, but his empathy showed nothing but a raw, hungry emptiness. Jay nearly fell backward as he was struck by the intensity of hunger, thirst, and exhaustion.

The cat stood on its back legs in order to bump its head against the playtime slave's hand, but the human stumbled and nearly fell at the pressure. He was trying to stay standing, because he wasn't supposed to fall down, but he was so very tired.

Cat, playtime slave needs food and water, Jay said.

Needs to play!

Later! Jay snapped back, making the cat hiss at him again.

Stupid slave.

The cat stalked off.

"Hello," Jay said. "Is anyone else up here waiting for something to eat?"

The slave answered with a hoarse voice, "There are others."

"Go downstairs to the kitchen," Jay said. "Get yourself something to eat and drink while I find the others. Can you make it down the stairs on your own?"

The slave hesitated, and then nodded. His mind was so odd, nearly empty. Despite his awareness of his physical needs—he probably hadn't eaten since Pet had been thrown out, more than twenty-four hours ago—he had no inclination to alleviate his own suffering. He had been able to open the door that would allow him into the kitchen this whole time, but hadn't done so until someone had knocked.

Slaves, Cat told him. *Not human people.*

Everyone is a slave to a cat, Jay commented.

Every person is a slave to a cat, Cat agreed, *but these are different. They don't have people-thoughts anymore. Only slave-thoughts. They don't play when they want to play and sleep when they want to sleep. They don't want anything.*

Jay wanted to argue, but Cat was right. His empathy sought impulses and images, wants and feelings, more than thoughts. These poor creatures didn't have impulses anymore. All independent, self-aware thought had been stripped from them.

Humans had enslaved humans, but they had never been able to destroy each other's minds and spirits the way a vampiric trainer could. No wonder Rikai had been so certain a slave couldn't be unbroken.

Maybe the Shantel elemental knew a way.

Maybe Rikai had been wrong; maybe the elemental even knew a way to destroy the new Midnight. Looking at these poor, destroyed creatures, Jay's determination to fight that sick empire burned even hotter.

First, though, he needed to get out of here. Before he could do that, he needed to know who *else* knew he was here. If Brina had come for him without mentioning her intent to others of her kind, Jay could probably kill her without anyone else ever knowing she had claimed him. If she *had* told someone else in Midnight, however, they might pursue that claim once Brina was dead—and then, Jay suspected, he would end up in a trainer's hands.

Against Brina, he was confident of his fighting abilities, but Midnight's trainers had been known to take witches who had come to kill them, snap their minds like kindling, and send them back to kill their own kin. If Jay had to face one of them, he wanted backup—*not* to be locked in a house with doors that wouldn't open, and windows that might or might not break.

It was time to talk to Brina.

A quick search made it clear that Brina wasn't on the second floor but did reveal yet another staircase, leading to an elegant set of French doors, which swung open easily when Jay tried them.

Brina's studio took his breath away—literally. Jay's eyes instantly watered in response to the fumes. He was glad he was hardier than a human.

The entire floor was a single room, with only a few columns

to interrupt the flow. Large windows and skylights, some cur-
tained and some open, would allow sunlight to stream into the
room during the day.

He started to explore but didn't get far before he found
the mistress of the house sprawled beneath a canvas in a pool
of black paint. His first thought was that she *had* recently been
suicidal, and it was possible that she may have figured out a
more effective method to use than hanging.

Would he get blamed for that?

If he could get out—

Brina stirred, and some power within or around her assaulted him with a blast of pure fury and anguish that made his
vision blacken and sent him to his hands and knees, retching.

A second blow made him shake and start to crawl to her
side. God, the pain . . .

Another blast, and he realized the anger he was feeling was
being channeled through Brina, but it wasn't from her. It was
someone, something else. Something powerful.

It hit him again, and he collapsed on top of Brina, who was
now whispering softly to herself. She was only semiconscious
at most, and wasn't speaking English. Jay thought the words
were French, but her thoughts were completely lost behind the
power that was latched on to her, tearing at her, draining her
in an effort to preserve itself.

The last time he had tried to help a damsel in distress, it
had ended with him dragged to Brina's home as a slave. He
tried to consider this situation a little more carefully, but he
couldn't consider, couldn't *think* with so much noise. He fought

to craft a bubble of protective power around them, struggling as each new blow made his whole body ache.

Please, just make it stop.

Rage and flames. It took everything he had just to hold on to the shield he had built, and to Brina, as the magic punched and pulled at them, making the air thick and scalding. It became impossible to draw a breath. He shuddered as his vision blackened, and his skin seemed to char, and at last . . .

He was walking through the black woods again. The brambles were gone, replaced by ferns and graceful vines with deep purple flowers. Large felines of all colors—white, tan, russet, brown, and black, solid and spotted—stalked through the forest around him, their footfalls soundless on the rich brown soil.

A woman was standing before him. Her body was dark like a shadow in night itself, beyond even the ink-black skin of the Shantel witch, without the white markings.

"Mind-witch." When she spoke, her voice was the rustling of the trees and the wind and the flowers. He needed no introduction to know he was standing before an avatar of the elemental that had once protected the Shantel.

"Are you the one attacking us now?" he asked.

"Attack you? Never. You freed my sakkri *from her prison,"* the elemental said. *"And now you've called to me to ask for my protection. I am willing to grant it."*

"I called to you?"

"I felt your power. Do you wish me to protect you?"

"How would you protect me?" he asked.

"*I will lend you my power. It will keep you safe when the fire withdraws.*"

"I don't understand."

"*Don't you?*" She looked up as if she heard something. "*I am at battle, and I must return to it. Do you wish to live?*"

"Of course I—"

"*Then do you accept my aid? I can protect you, or I can end you now and spare your suffering.*"

"What is going *on*?"

"*Choose now, witch. Do you accept my aid?*"

He drew an uncertain breath, then said, "I want to live. If your aid is the only way to do that, then yes, I accept."

"*Very well.*"

CHAPTER 16

THE HEAT WITHDREW abruptly, leaving him shivering in Brina's studio. The deep blackness of the moonless evening seemed infinitely colder than it had been before.

Beneath him, Brina gasped. Her body was nearly convulsing in its struggles to warm itself. Her breath came in ragged gasps, and her heart pounded.

Wait . . . that wasn't right.

Vampires' hearts didn't *beat*. They didn't need to breathe, much less gasp.

"Brina?" he whispered.

Her eyes opened wide, and they were a brilliant, clear blue, no longer the pure black of a vampire.

"What has happened?" she asked with a trembling voice. She rose to her feet, then promptly fainted in his arms.

Jay could feel her heart pounding so quickly that he was worried it was going to burst. Could it? He had no idea how much strain was suddenly on her body.

He barked orders to the other slaves on his way out of Brina's studio, commanding them to take care of themselves until he returned. He didn't dare take them to SingleEarth yet. He didn't know how to save them, and didn't want to endanger anyone else through yet *another* impulsive action.

Maybe Brina could help him help them, after she recovered. She had to know more about Midnight than anyone but a vampire could possibly know.

What is *she now?*

Why am I trying to save her?

Mine! the cat objected, when Jay carried Brina down the stairs. He prayed as he reached for the door, and was relieved when it opened without resistance, probably cued to Brina's needs. The cat followed them both out into the snow, keeping up a litany of complaints about the snow, the cold, and why Brina and Jay were ignoring him. It was doubly offended when Jay wouldn't let it into the car.

Jay settled Brina's unconscious body into a calmer state before driving as quickly as he sanely could back to Haven #2.

She will *wake up eventually. What are you going to do with her then?*

What would have happened if he hadn't interfered? Would Brina be dead now? How many others had this happened to?

Brina hadn't felt like the elemental's primary focus. For all Jay knew, the trainers had just been wiped from the map.

Could ending Midnight be so simple?

Thoughts swirling, he pulled into the clinic's parking lot at dawn and lifted Brina in his arms. Haven #2 was primarily a medical facility, so they didn't have many vampires, but if Jay could get in touch with Xeke . . . Or, what if Xeke was hurt, too? Jay knew Xeke didn't condone Midnight, but he had some connection to it. Would the elemental be able to tell the difference?

"I need some help!" Jay shouted, flagging down a nurse as he crossed the threshold of the medical building. As soon as Brina was safe, he could call Xeke.

"Put her here," the nurse said, gesturing to one of those rolling beds, which had been left in the hall. "What's going on?"

"I think she . . ." He trailed off as he checked out the nurse. She smelled of antiseptic and gardenia perfume, and her name tag said *Volunteer.* She was probably perfectly capable as a nurse, but Jay didn't want to dump on her the impossibility of a centuries-old vampire being revived. "She was having a heart attack," he said. "Is Caryn here?"

The wide-eyed volunteer nodded as she lifted the safety rails on the bed. "Is she able to be transferred to a human hospital?" she asked. "A heart attack is more acute than our clinic usually—"

"No, she isn't," Jay interrupted. He glanced at Brina, not wanting to leave her, but he needed to talk to someone of higher authority. "I'll go find Caryn. You should do whatever medical things you do for someone having a heart attack," he said. "My magic put her out, though, so don't be worried that she won't wake up right away."

He didn't wait for her response but sought out Caryn, who was just finishing an exam with a smiling, pregnant shapeshifter. Since the patient obviously wasn't in immediate distress, Jay didn't hesitate to pull Caryn aside to say, "I need your help."

"You're back!" Caryn said. By this point, Jay was almost starting to get used to his empathy being a burned-out blur, but Caryn's relief was so obvious on her face that even he could recognize it. "Are you okay?"

"Yes, fine," he replied shortly. "But I need you to look in on the woman I brought back with me." He chewed his lip, not knowing how to begin. "It's Brina."

Caryn's eyes widened. "Brina the vampire? Have you alerted the—"

"No, no, it's not a matter for hunters," he interrupted. "She's unconscious. And she's human." He cut off all questions, speaking rapidly. "I don't know how. But I need to find out, which means I need to leave Brina here. I have no idea what kind of shape she's in physically. Can you keep her safe and unconscious until I get back?"

Caryn nodded. Softly, she asked, "Jay, how much trouble are you in?"

"Hey, there's a chance I might not be in any trouble at all," he replied optimistically. "Wouldn't that be nice?"

Caryn looked openly skeptical, but all she said was "I'll check on Brina, and if it's safe, I'll sedate her. Then—" She broke off with a sneeze. "That new volunteer's perfume should be outlawed."

"I think she's taking Brina's vitals right now, so you'll get another good whiff of her," Jay teased, earning a halfhearted glare. "But really, thanks. I'll be back as soon as I can."

It was a little past dawn, an hour when most vampires were settling down to sleep, but Jay returned to his room and tried to call Sarah anyway. Nikolas and Kristopher were close to Kendra, who most certainly *was* allied with Midnight, and the same vampire who had changed their sister Nissa had also changed Brina. They hadn't been alive during Midnight's first reign, but would the elemental know—or care—about that difference?

"*Allô, c'est Marguerite.*"

"Um . . . Hi, this is Jay. Sarah's cousin?" He hoped he had the right number. "Is Nikolas available?" Sarah was almost certainly asleep for the day already, but the older vampire might still be awake.

"*Non*, no, he is sleeping. Is there a message?"

If his bloodbond didn't know of a problem, then Nikolas was *probably* fine. But *probably* wasn't enough to settle Jay's anxiety. "Could you check on him?"

"Is there a reason to be concerned?" Intriguing. Marguerite's French accent disappeared as worry crept in.

"A magical . . . thing," Jay answered vaguely. "Probably nothing, but—"

He broke off, because he heard a door open on the other end of the line, followed by soft voices. When Marguerite spoke next, she no longer sounded friendly. "He is fine. Is there anything else?" The accent was creeping back in. Was it something she did intentionally? It would be a great way to divert solicitors.

"No, I— Actually, wait. Do you know anything about Midnight?" Marguerite had been around a long time.

"*Très peu.*"

Jay had no idea what that meant, but he was pretty sure that the sudden return to French was her way of evading the question.

"If the vampiric mistress of a household is indisposed, can someone help her slaves without getting in trouble?" he pressed, thinking of the people he had left behind at Brina's house.

No answer, for long enough that Jay glanced at his phone to check that he was in fact still connected. "Marguerite?"

"It would be . . . inadvisable for you to do such a thing," she replied. "Midnight's laws are not charitable toward someone of your vocation."

"What if someone else from SingleEarth did it, someone who isn't a hunter?"

"No, no," she snapped. "Any mortal would be seen as a thief. Their freedom would be forfeit."

That advice might have been helpful *before* Jay had walked off with the *sakkri.* "But what if—"

"If I ask Nikolas to look into this," Marguerite interrupted, "will you cease these questions?"

Jay trusted Nikolas to take care of the helpless people in Brina's household, and Marguerite wouldn't have offered anything that could get her cherished master in trouble. "It's Brina's slaves I'm worried about," he said. "I have reason to believe she may not be returning home soon."

"If she is dead, Nikolas cannot interfere with inheritance laws." Marguerite's voice went soft, and perfectly neutral.

It was a reasonable assumption to make, but in this case it brought a somewhat hysterical laugh from his throat. "No, not dead," he gasped out. *Quite the opposite.*

"Then I will speak with Nikolas when he wakes. Can I assure him that you do not intend to do anything stupid? He and Sarah have expressed concern for you."

"Anything stupid" was a broad, poorly defined category. "You can let him know I got home safely, and that I trust him to help Brina's slaves so I don't need to do anything stupid about *them.*"

"*Ça suffit.*"

"Great."

He hung up, feeling no more comforted than before. Nikolas was fine. That was good, but what did it *mean*? Had the elemental targeted only her most recent captor? Or targeted only slave traders, or trainers?

Rikai. She had contacts galore, and understood sorcery.

The three-hour drive to Rikai's home was frustrating to the extreme. He wasn't sure she would be willing to meet with him once he arrived, but he didn't have a phone number to call. His hopes and fears both rose as he drove into the driveway and found Rikai standing on her front step, one hand braced on the doorframe, her foot tapping. She had known he was coming.

"We need to talk again, witch," she said, "in a little more detail."

She sounded out of breath, and as he approached, he realized her posture was not casual at all. She was standing stiffly, as if in pain.

"What happened to you?" he asked, reaching out instinctively with his power—and then retreating as he felt her magic snatch at his hungrily.

She smiled, though the expression never reached her eyes. "Do you stick your hand in tiger cages, too?"

"Did someone attack you?"

"Right now I'm more concerned with what has happened to *you*," she replied. "I have a feeling that you have had an interesting couple of days. Walk with me, and tell me, what—exactly—did the Shantel elemental say when it spoke to you?"

"Um . . ." He followed Rikai back to her study, trying to find the right words. Rikai didn't seem to notice his hesitation as she walked with a tightly controlled stride, not limping but obviously trying to conceal an injury of some sort.

"Well?" Rikai prompted as she settled into one of those ominous chairs and gestured for him to do the same.

"It said it was going to destroy Midnight," Jay admitted.

"Exactly that?" Rikai asked.

"I think—" He broke off. What exactly *had* it said? *She will be all I need to destroy those who hurt her.* "Well, it said it would destroy those who hurt her. Which *is* Midnight, right?"

Rikai took a deep, bracing breath, and then let it out in a slow stream.

"A few hours ago," Jay said, trying to get all the information out before Rikai responded, "something happened to Brina. I went to her, and I heard the elemental again, and it offered to protect me. When whatever was happening was over, Brina was human."

Rikai quirked a brow, but her next question wasn't for Jay. Rather, she picked up her phone and dialed a number. When the line picked up, she didn't waste time with pleasantries. She just asked, "Is Xeke all right?"

Jay couldn't hear the reply, but Rikai nodded thoughtfully. After she hung up, she said simply, "He's dead. Now, we—"

"*Dead?*" Jay interrupted, feeling his stomach drop. He hadn't intended . . . And Rikai, sitting there like it didn't matter . . . *I have to call Sarah.* If Xeke was dead, then what about—

"*Still* dead," Rikai clarified, with an impatient wave of her hand, "as opposed to alive and human. He *is* a vampire, after all. His partner says he is fine. Get a grip."

Trying to swallow the panic that hadn't yet subsided, Jay stammered, "Well, um, g-good. That's . . ." He took a deep breath. Had she done that intentionally? "What is going on?"

"I would like to examine Brina."

"And I would like you to answer me!" Jay snapped anxiously.

"Of course you would, but unlike you, I try not to blather answers until I know what they are. Now, where did you leave Brina?"

"SingleEarth," Jay answered, resigned.

"Excellent," Rikai said. "I'll get my tools, and then we will go."

CHAPTER 17

BRINA WOKE FEELING disoriented, thirsty, and heavy. Sunlight was streaming in through a nearby window, and there was a rushing sound in her ears, impossibly loud. Standing up took a monumental effort, as if she were moving the weight of a small building.

Her gown started to slip off her shoulders, and she snatched at it with confusion before realizing that someone had undone the buttons down the back. She couldn't do them back up on her own, and standing there clutching brocade was hardly dignified, so she shimmied out of the heavy gown and stood in only her chemise. She could breathe more easily that way, anyway.

Why am I breathing?

She tried holding her breath, but doing so made her dizzy, and made her chest and head hurt. When she stopped struggling not to, her body automatically kept breathing, as if it always had.

The rushing, pounding, slamming, overpowering noise in her ears, then . . . was that her *heart*?

She swallowed. Her throat was sore, and she was . . . *hungry*. She didn't like being hungry. It reminded her of days she didn't like to think about.

Brina stalked to the door, which was standing open. Where was she? Someone had brought her here, and made her alive, and they wouldn't have done so without anticipating that she would need them.

The pretty witch!

She smiled, and then frowned, as she recalled him. He had been kind to her at the party, but then he had stolen Pet. Then he had agreed to help her in Pet's place, and then—

Something had happened after that. It had been like people screaming and shoving her from all directions, ripping at her, furious and terrified. Somewhere in the chaos she had seen the witch.

He had brought her here.

He would help her.

But there was no one in the hallway to bring him to her.

Her chemise was more decent than many outfits modern girls wore, but Brina still stepped gingerly into the hallway, wishing she had another option. Her bare feet were cold, and she mentally added slippers to the list of things she wanted as she put on a proud face and tried to pretend she didn't feel frightened, hungry, and half naked.

Most of the rooms she passed were occupied by sleeping people. Eventually, though, she found a large room that might have once been a ballroom or a gymnasium. It had been decorated for Christmas, but the unlit tree and bright decorations had been shoved aside to make room for a makeshift sick ward. Effort had been made to keep the ill comfortable, but blankets and pillows could not conceal their restless movements or the stench of their sweat.

Nurses circled like buzzards picking at the ill.

The world rushed around Brina as she looked around, and the pounding of her heart in her ears became louder and more rapid. There wasn't enough air in this room, and what air there was she couldn't draw into her lungs fast enough. There were so many here, coughing and gasping and calling for help.

She didn't want to faint again. She fought against it; her knuckles went white as she gripped the doorframe, struggling to stay standing.

"Can I help you?" someone asked, taking her arm.

Brina shook her head, and at the same time she asked, "What is this plague?"

The human winced, and said, "It's the *flu*. We think it may even be the one this year's flu shot protects against, since none of the humans have it." As she spoke, she touched Brina's brow and the back of her neck. "How do you feel?"

"Cold," Brina admitted. "Horrified. There are so many."

"I know it's normally considered rude to ask at SingleEarth, but . . . what are you?"

Brina blinked at her, startled. "I'm . . . not sure right now."

"Not sure?"

"I imagine that's why I was brought here."

"Then you could be at risk," the nurse said. "If you're not already ill, you shouldn't be here. You'll be exposed."

"I've had the plague before," Brina whispered.

"Then maybe you're—" The human broke off, frowned, and finally asked, "I'm sorry, are you a resident here?"

Brina wasn't listening anymore. She needed to see what was happening.

She followed meandering paths through the sick, taking note of all the colors around her. Onyx hair, fair skin, and eyes like emeralds. It wasn't the fever that made the skin seem pearlescent and the eyes that tracked her movement with dazed hope look like polished gems; it was the distinctive coloration of a serpent shapeshifter. At another pallet, she glimpsed feathers beneath the sweat-matted hair of a young boy whose brown hair and hazel eyes suggested he was probably a sparrow. Next, a mane of rich auburn, shorn short—a fox, a rare breed to find out of their enclave.

Brina had hundreds of years of practice; she knew how to recognize an individual's breed and state of health at sight. She wouldn't have paid a pence for any of these pitiful creatures if they had been human, and since they weren't, they shouldn't have been in this condition. Only magic could do this to the nonhuman.

At the next bed, she found a young woman who was kneeling to tend the sick. Her head was bowed and her hands were splayed in front of her on the floor, as if that was all that was keeping her from toppling over on top of the unconscious shapeshifter in front of her.

"Whose spell is it?" Brina asked.

"Spell?" the kneeling girl echoed, without seeming to comprehend.

Brina resisted the urge to kick the girl to get her attention, but only because doing so would probably knock her over. Instead, she said as clearly as possible, "Yes, spell. They cannot just be *sick*."

Saying the word drove another chill through her, brought a memory of a wailing baby. She pushed it away. Now wasn't the time.

There is no good time to remember that day.

"They *are* sick," the girl snapped in response. She shoved herself to her feet, only to stumble and nearly fall. Brina jumped back, narrowly eluding the woman's fever-hot hands as she sought some way to balance herself.

The would-be healer glared at Brina with blue eyes that then widened as she said, "Brina." Before Brina could correct her, the girl said, "Lady Brina. Whatever you call yourself. You should be sleeping. I put you to sleep. Used my power."

"You do not look like you have the power to put a mouse to sleep," Brina observed. The girl must have fancied herself a witch, one of those who supposedly ran this SingleEarth place. "Tell me what has happened to me, and what has happened here, before you faint." The girl's face was already pale, and her lips had that cerulean hue that suggested unconsciousness was imminent.

"Caryn, you shouldn't be up," another voice said. Brina bristled as a young man pushed his way past her, jostling her without apology as he hurried to take the sick witch into his arms.

"I need to *do* something," the girl responded.

"Your fever is back," the solicitous young man said.

"Can't focus my magic," Caryn whispered, leaning her head on his shoulder.

"Some of the shapeshifters are responding to human medication. I know you said these medications don't normally do anything for your kind, but you're going to try."

She nodded, but then added, "Only treats the symptoms."

"The symptoms are boiling your brain," Brina interjected. "You need a witch."

"I *am* a witch!" the girl snapped, showing previously unseen spirit.

"You're a useless witch," Brina replied.

"Who are *you*?" the boy demanded.

"I am Lady Brina di'Birgetta," she replied, drawing up to her full height. "In the last day, I have had my property stolen and been assaulted in my own home, and now I've been abducted and brought to this plague ward against my will. I have been as patient as I intend to be, and now I demand to know what is going on."

The boy just stared at her.

"Are you simple?" she asked.

"She's a vampire," the little witch whispered to him. "Or was. Jay brought her in."

"Jay," the boy answered, shaking his head. "He—" He broke off, his face going pale as he asked slowly, "May I ask what century?"

"Not the time for historical curiosity," Caryn chastised him.

"When were you changed? Please, um, my lady. It may help me answer your questions."

"The year 1665," Brina answered. How was that relevant?

After drawing a deep breath, he asked, "Europe?"

"Italy."

"Nurse!" Brina jumped as the young man raised his voice to call to yet another man across the room. "We need to get her quarantined and onto antibiotics. The flu is bad enough in a population without a single antibody. I don't know what happens when a vampire turns human, and I don't want to test it. From that era, you could be carrying the goddamned bubonic plague."

Brina wasn't listening any longer, not since he had said the word *quarantine.*

Deaf to anything but the heartbeat in her ears, she slammed an elbow into the stomach of the first nurse stupid enough to touch her. The doctor had lied to her, had told her he could help her, just to get the information he would use to imprison her.

She fought tooth and nail, but she was *weak.* Pathetic.

Human doctors and nurses swarmed, irreverent and immoral, intent on trapping her again, confining her with the dead and dying—

She twisted her head with a snarl as she felt a sharp pinch in the meat of her arm. She looked just in time to see the needle in her flesh. Her previous weakness was nothing compared to the way her body now seemed to collapse, her innards folding into origami. Flowers and paper cranes, made of swirling colors and fancy lights.

Foolish girl, something whispered to her as she sank into a drugged sleep. *Even more frightened of life than you are of dying. I should hate you . . . but I suppose I must credit you with hiding my child away, when the hunters would have murdered her. You gave me time. So I will give you time.*

Time for what? Brina tried to ask. But the words wouldn't form.

CHAPTER 18

As HE DROVE, the pain that Jay could sense coming from Rikai gradually built, until it was taking all his concentration to ignore it and focus on the slick roads. She hadn't said a word or uttered as much as a grunt, but a few miles out from Single-Earth, Jay couldn't stand it anymore.

"What is *wrong* with you?" he demanded.

"That remains to be seen," she replied, voice perfectly level. All Jay knew about Triste magic was that it relied on total control of mind and body, regardless of pain or other physical ailments. That made it doubly concerning when Rikai's next words—"We need to . . ."—faded out, replaced by a sharp hitch of breath. "Let me know when we arrive."

Out of the corner of his eye, he saw her rest her head on

her hands on the window. He resisted the urge to drive faster, knowing that a patch of ice and a car accident could kill him just as surely as magical influences.

Why wouldn't she *talk* to him? Was her pain related to what had happened to Brina?

His questions about Rikai were pushed aside by more pressing concerns as he reached SingleEarth and discovered that the parking lot was overflowing. Cars were parked wherever they could find space, many blocking others in.

"Looks like they're having a party," he said, feigning levity to cover his rising anxiety. "We're going to have to hike a bit." Jay stopped the car as close as he could get to the main building.

For the first time in hours, he got a good look at Rikai. Her face was pale and there were shadows under her eyes. More disturbing were the ropy scars he could see trailing out from her shirt cuffs to cover her hands. Another was starting to emerge from beneath her high collar, snaking up the left side of her throat to her temple.

He clenched his jaw against the echo of her pain and walked around the car to open her door. Rikai glared at him, as if she wanted to refuse his help, but then she reached up and took his arm. She leaned on him heavily as they began an agonizingly long walk to the door.

Halfway there, Lynx came bounding across the snow, his tufted ears back as if he had scented something foul.

What happened here? Jay asked.

Stinks like something spoiled, Lynx answered. *Stay out here.*

I need to go in to find out what happened.

Lynx hissed, and refused to follow as Jay and Rikai approached the threshold of SingleEarth Haven #2.

"What the hell?" Jay whispered as he stepped inside and discovered that the reception area had been turned into a triage unit. Nurses and volunteers were scampering among patients who had been laid out on blankets, towels, even yoga mats, while other workers made hushed phone calls desperately calling for more doctors. Though they struggled to appear professional, the panicky fear rising from the staff left a bitter taste on Jay's tongue.

One of them glanced up, barely seemed to register his presence, and said, "Sign her in at the front desk. We're trying to find space for everyone."

"I need to put you down," Jay said, warning Rikai but not asking her permission as he dropped the Triste and knelt next to the nearest patient. Rikai stumbled before she found her balance, but at that moment, Jay couldn't have cared less if she fell.

The patient had previously been a receptionist at this haven. Jay couldn't recall her name, but he knew she was a leopard shapeshifter. She shouldn't have been able to get sick, but the moment he touched her, he could feel the illness racing through her.

"Jay." He looked up when Jeremy whispered his name. "You shouldn't be here. The shapeshifters are getting it worst, but witches aren't"—*Oh, god, how did I let her get that bad before I noticed?*—"aren't immune." Jeremy's voice hitched in the middle, and Jay's heart leapt into his throat at the image that came along with the human's hesitation: Caryn fainting, her fever 102 degrees and climbing.

"Caryn's sick?"

Jeremy nodded. "Her mother and aunt, too."

"Vireo?"

"Not as bad as some of the others, but he started sniffling a couple hours ago. How are you feeling?" Jeremy reached forward as he spoke, but Jay was barely aware of the human touching his brow and taking his pulse. "You're chilled."

"We had to walk in the snow to get here," Jay snapped, jerking back. "Where's my brother?"

"He went with a busload of patients to Center Number Twelve," Jeremy answered. "They have more resources, so those well enough to travel have moved. Caryn's still here," he added, a note of desperation breaking into his voice as he fought an internal battle with himself. *If he tries to help, he could get sick. He needs to help. I can't ask it of him.*

"Where is she?" Jay asked.

Jeremy didn't have the willpower to say any of the sensible things he knew he should say as a doctor, and that was good, because Jay didn't have patience for an argument. He was already trembling as they entered Caryn's room and he caught the first reek of fever-sweat.

Caryn's eyes opened but didn't focus. She was flushed, and her hair was matted.

"Jay?" she asked. Her voice was hoarse. "No, stay back. You'll catch it."

Jay flinched. Jeremy had said nearly the same thing, but all

Jay had felt was his concern for Caryn. Suddenly Jay could feel the creeping fog of the illness, and for the first time, a more personal terror seeped in.

What if I'm *sick?* Jay wondered. *Would I notice?* He was struggling against exhaustion and panic. He felt like he had been kicked in the gut and then punched a few times. Was that just fear, or some microscopic malady?

He forced himself to Caryn's side and took her hand. Humans got sick all the time, and they were still brave enough to work in hospitals, or even retail locations or schools where disease was easily passed on. Jay refused to be too much of a coward to approach his own cousin.

"Control yourself, witch," Rikai hissed as Jay paused again, pushing back the black spots that tried to claim his vision. "You're not ill. Control your breath, and you will force your body to calm. You need to be calm."

Jay had lost track of Rikai in the face of this pestilence. Jeremy asked sharply, "Who is this?"

"Never mind me. Try to help your cousin," Rikai prompted Jay. For a moment, he thought she was being compassionate, but then he realized that she was gazing at Caryn like a scientist dissecting a rat.

Jay turned all his focus on his cousin and the snarled energies within her. It had been easy to encourage Jeremy's human immune system to respond to an invading illness, but Caryn's body had never needed to fight off disease. It didn't know how. He did what he could for her, but then he needed to pull his magic away or risk doing more harm than good. He was struggling to put her into a deep, healing sleep, when someone in the hall shouted. Jay didn't catch the words, but he felt the lash of fresh anxiety like a slap.

Jeremy turned gray. Shot to his feet. Froze. Stared at Caryn. Turned toward the door.

Turned back and grabbed Jay's arm. "Come," he ordered, dragging Jay after him.

The human's emotions had gone beyond anything Jay could comprehend. They were grayed-out in panic, and the only explanation Jay had was the echoes of "Code blue!" that the nurses in the hall were still calling.

"What does that—"

Jay didn't get the question out before he and Jeremy were in another room, this one crowded with confused and over-whelmed medical staff. The volunteer with the gardenia perfume was sitting in the corner, her knees up at her chest, her mind echoing with a single, looping thought: *This doesn't happen here.*

"Get out of the *way!*" Jeremy shouted, pushing volunteers aside and trying to decide if anyone else in the room had ever been trained for—

This. Jay finally saw the shapeshifter on the bed. He hadn't realized she was there before, because she was dead.

Jeremy was trying to give CPR, thinking, *We're not equipped for this kind of crisis here.* And, *Jay, if your magic can help, now is the time.*

Jay couldn't help with *dead.* Could anyone help with *dead?* Jeremy seemed to think Jay could.

"I can't."

He backed out of the room, running into Rikai, who had followed like a shadow once again. As his hand brushed hers, her pain slipped past his already strained shields. Not just now-pain. Memories. Stretching, falling, wrenching, burning, stabbing, slicing . . . and she had been so innocent then, so young.

And now her body was riddled with enough scar tissue that it was remarkable she could walk. Her power was still holding some of the worst injuries back, but it was taking all her energy to do so.

She yanked her hand and power away from his with a glare, as he gasped, "I'm sorry. How—"

He didn't finish asking the question, because the answer came to him: Inquisition. Most of Jay's ancestors had managed to flee the church's deadly fire, but this woman had been caught in it. She had still been human. Worse, she had once been absolutely faithful to the church. She was one of the rare few the inquisitors had never broken. She had been certain that lying to stop the pain would damn her forever, and so she had never confessed, never named the names they'd demanded in order to make the pain stop.

Jay gagged, trying to shove her memories away, trying to push aside the panic the nurses and volunteers and people who worked here were feeling because normally witches dealt with the scary cases and everything else was okay. Jay ran from the poor little nurse who was doing her best to take over for Jeremy, though she was thinking, *This is why I left New York?*

Back down the hallway.

Block out the fear, the fever dreams, the shuddering weakness, the—

Rikai grabbed his hands, and pain shot through him like lightning—but this time it was intentionally given, not accidentally shared. It cut through the emotions he couldn't seem to block out, and momentarily cleared his mind.

"You. Need. To. Focus," she snapped. "You—"

A faint buzz interrupted her. Letting go of one of his hands, Rikai reached into her pocket and retrieved a slim flip phone, which she opened with clumsy, stiff fingers. "Yes?"

Her expression never changed as she listened for a few moments, but she dropped Jay's other hand as she said, "Pick me up from SingleEarth Haven Number Two."

She closed the phone, looked at Jay, and said, "My power comes in part from the same elemental who gives us all our magic, but beyond Leona, I have made deals with entities darker than your deepest fears. If Xeke dies, and you are responsible, then know I will see you devoured by creatures you cannot begin to comprehend."

"Xeke's sick?" Jay asked. How could a *vampire* get sick? Unless he was like Brina. Jay hadn't even thought of her since arriving. Was she sick, too? He should check on her.

Rikai shook her head. "He is as he has been, but he feeds and feeds and cannot staunch the bloodlust. He nearly killed his lover this evening when he woke."

"Please," Jay whispered. "If you have any idea what is happening—if you can *help*—you need to tell me."

"I should think it would be perfectly obvious," Rikai replied infuriatingly.

"Well, it's *not!*" The only thing that was obvious was that she was standing in the middle of a sick ward that could too easily turn into a morgue, and she didn't seem to care.

"Fine. The elemental you helped, the one you thought offered to attack Midnight, has chosen to start a little higher on the chain of command than the slave traders or the trainers," Rikai answered. "The Shantel elemental isn't going after vampires. She's going after *Leona.*"

"I don't understand."

Rikai laughed, but the sharp, barking sound barely seemed to indicate amusement. "You probably don't want to understand, little witch. Because if *I* understand right, you caused this." She made a sweeping gesture encompassing all the chaos around them. "You'll live through it, as long as you stay out of the way. The Shantel elemental has marked you, and her power will protect you. But when elementals war, civilizations *burn.*"

I didn't want this, Jay thought desperately as Rikai turned on her heel and headed toward the door. *Please. I didn't want any of this.*

CHAPTER 19

A WAILING BABY. People coughing. Red blood left behind on a white handkerchief.

I will get us out of here. I swear to you, I will get us out of here.

You're dead, Daryl. You can't help me now.

Brina woke with a violent shudder, hoping to discover that the entire previous day had been nothing but a surreal nightmare.

No such blessing.

She opened her eyes to find herself back in her tiny, sterile room. The smell of antiseptic stung her nose, and the lingering drugs had left her mouth dry and her head foggy. Wisps of dreams and memories kept seeping into the waking world, confusing her further.

Angelica, please don't cry.

Brina couldn't get the memory of that baby's wail out of her head. At the end, of course, it hadn't been a wail but rather a wheeze, as little Angelica's skin had darkened and—

No! Don't think of that.

Brina stared at the door, summoning the courage to stand and try to open it. She didn't want to know if it was locked and guarded.

Let the birds sing, dilly, dilly, and the lambs play.

They put chains on the doors. Painted red. Guards outside.

We shall be safe, dilly, dilly, out of harm's way.

She was going mad.

Last time, Daryl had saved them. He had told her that he'd bribed the guards to leave their posts, but Brina suspected he had killed them. She hadn't ever asked him, and certainly hadn't blamed him. It was the only way they could have gotten out as anything other than corpses. The plague had already taken Mother, Father, the maid, and finally little baby Angelica, who had died in Brina's arms. Daryl had done what he'd needed to do. He always had.

Brina stood and started toward the door, stumbling when her head spun from the abrupt movement. She touched the cold doorknob, twisted it, and yanked so hard that she nearly fell when it opened. She hadn't expected it to.

Once it had, she wasn't sure what to do. People were shouting, coughing, and crying all around her.

She took a step forward and spied a familiar figure down the hall, but stopped when she realized he had tears on his pale face. Her witch. What was his name?

He turned and saw her. Relief and shock battled on his face as he hurried to her side, reaching out to her. She dove into his arms, remembering how comforting they had been last time he had held her. This time, though, his breath was fast and his heart was pounding.

"B-Brina," he breathed. "I'm sorry. I never meant to have you wake up alone, but I didn't ever imagine this. . . ." He trailed off, and then said, "You shouldn't be exposed to this."

"Exposed?" Brina echoed, aware that her voice was shrill as she lifted her head.

Jay touched her face, lifting her chin so she was looking directly at him. "You're hungry," he said. "I'll get you something to eat, and then we'll figure out what—"

"Don't talk to me like I'm a child!" Brina shouted, loud enough that she startled even herself as she shoved against his chest. He was as bad as Kaleo. "I am *not* an infant. I want to know what is going on here, and why, and I want to know what you did to me, and I want to know when you're going to put things back the way they were."

There. She put her hands on her hips and stared down at him. A true lady knew how to look down at *anyone*, even a man a foot taller.

He stared at her with no little surprise. She prepared herself for him to try to dismiss her questions again, as if coddling her could make her ignore everything going on around them, but he didn't. He spoke carefully, obviously struggling to get the words out past his own emotions.

"I don't fully understand what power made you human,"

the witch said, "and I don't know how to undo it. Something is happening right now that is causing power and magic to change. A lot of people are in trouble."

"That is a great many unknowns," she responded. "*What* is happening right now?"

The witch flinched, his gaze averting. Even Brina could recognize guilt when she saw it so blatantly displayed. He blamed himself for what was going on. Was he right?

"Shapeshifters and witches are sick," Brina said, trying to start the story for him. "Did you do a spell?"

"No!" he shouted, the protest echoing through the hall. "No," he repeated. "I just wanted to help someone. I—" His voice quieted, until in a wavering whisper he asked, "What do you know about your, um, housemaid? Who she used to be?"

Was he trying to distract her? No. He was too serious.

"She was a witch and a shapeshifter," Brina answered. "I never saw any evidence of special power, though she must have some. Only the magic-users can live so long." She frowned. "*She* caused this plague?"

"Yes—no, not directly, I guess, but—" He shook his head, and admitted, "I don't understand elementals."

You gave me time. So I will give you time. Brina had thought those words had been a product of the drugs, but now she understood them. If Daryl had not taken command of Pet when he had, the once-*sakkri* would have died when Midnight had burned. Instead, Daryl had hidden her, intending to present her to Brina as a surprise that night. As a result, she was one of the only slaves who had survived the slaughter.

"Rikai said the Shantel elemental should be weak, but she was wrong, so wrong," Jay said, the words falling out of his mouth now like a boy at confession. "Whatever I did trying to help the shapeshifter made the Shantel elemental able to attack Leona. And that is making people sick. And I don't know what to do."

The last words were a pathetic whisper. A plea.

Brina's first instinct was to step back. No one had ever looked at her like that, desperately seeking an answer they both knew probably didn't exist. Ever since childhood, people had treated her as something that needed to be sheltered and indulged. Now this witch looked as if he would like to drop the weight of the world on her shoulders, if only it would help get some of the weight off his own.

"So." She didn't know what to do. Fine. She would do what she always did—pretend. Stand straight. Look proud. Speak confidently. "We need to fix this."

"It's not as easy as just wanting it done," he snapped. "The problem involves powers way beyond either of us. Elementals, battling."

Her arm flew of its own accord, responding to the shrill, panicked tone in his voice. After the sharp *crack* made by her palm against his cheek, he stared at her with obvious shock.

Now calm, and staring directly into her eyes, he said in a flat voice, "You are *not* allowed to hit me."

"Your actions may have triggered the destruction of your world," she replied. "Which, incidentally, is also *my* world. I will refrain from hitting you if you will refrain from self-indulgent pity and defeatism. Now, how do we find the fighting elementals?" she asked.

"Have you heard a word I've said?" he asked.

"I've heard you say it's *hard*," she retorted. "And I gather you would rather give up and trust your fate—as well as mine, and however many others'—to the winds of chance. Perhaps you have no chivalry or courage. If that's the case, tell me what you know, and I will do what I can. I will not be imprisoned in another house."

She would not wait this time and let fate choose whether she would live or die. Daryl was gone, and this witch needed to be saved.

It was up to her.

"Brina," Jay said hopelessly, "I want to help, but I don't know what to do. I don't even know where to *begin*. People I love are sick. My brother is sick, do you understand that? And I know it's my fault, but Rikai has already walked out on me, and I barely know anything about elementals or the Shantel."

Giving into instinct, she pulled him close, her holding him this time. His hair was softer than she had expected. She started to contemplate what colors she would need to re-create its silky shades and highlights, and then her mind reeled back in.

"I know about the Shantel," she said. Her stomach grumbled in a most unladylike way, making her blush and realize that she was hugging this man while wearing nothing but her shift. "I would appreciate it if you could assist me in dressing. Then we can share what knowledge we have. That is a good place to begin."

The witch nodded. She shied back from the light of gratitude in his eyes, and tried to conceal the uncomfortable moment as she returned to her room and gathered up the gown she had removed earlier. She pulled it over her head and settled the skirt into place, by which time the witch had come up behind her.

"This seems pretty tight," he said as he started to fasten the two dozen mother-of-pearl buttons that ran down the back of the dress. "Warn me if you have trouble breathing."

She nodded.

"Though I never met her before she was Pet, I knew *of* the *sakkri*," Brina said as Jay worked. He was right that the dress was snug, but she seemed to be able to draw enough air to sustain herself and continue speaking. "The Shantel did not like visitors, and attempting to trespass on their land was problematic, but they allowed us to pass through in exchange for certain trade agreements. It was an acceptable arrangement."

"Do you know much about how their magic works?" Jay asked.

She chewed her lip and considered. "The heart of their active magic is illusion," she said. "If you walk in the Shantel woods, they seem to change around you. Shantel hunters know exactly where you are, but you never see them until they wish it. No matter what compass you use, you end up where the magic wants you, whether that means outside their territory or at the Family Courtyard, which is what they call their palace."

"If Shantel magic is so strong," Jay asked as Brina began to finger-comb her hair into some semblance of presentable, "how did Midnight get its hands on the *sakkri*?"

The accusation in his tone was sharp enough to cut, but she raised her gaze, unflinching. "The same way all shapeshifters came to us. She was sold by her own kind. Humans used to send their criminals to Australia, or the Americas. Under Midnight, the shapeshifter nations used us for the same purpose. I do not know what crime a *sakkri* could perform that would merit such a punishment, but I assure you it was her people who made the choice—not mine."

Brina couldn't deny the many atrocities intrinsic to Midnight; they were why she had rarely gone to the main building unless she had needed to. The trainers were vicious animals whose only instinct was to destroy, and Mistress Jeshickah herself had the emotional depth of a jackal. But Midnight was the only game in town, and *everyone* played by its rules.

At least the Shantel elemental had one thing right: Mistress Jeshickah and her trainers were not the only ones responsible for everything the Shantel had suffered.

CHAPTER 20

NOW IS PROBABLY *not the time to argue,* Jay thought, biting back a retort. Maybe the Shantel had sold their *sakkri* into Midnight, and maybe they hadn't. Jay didn't know for sure.

"They sold her to Daryl?"

Idiot! You weren't going to discuss it—or him*!*

Brina flinched from her brother's name but approached the question. "A Shantel witch is too valuable to go to anyone but Jeshickah's chosen. If we could find the trainer who worked with her, he would know more about her magic. He would have studied it before accepting her."

He. Brina said *he* with more distaste and slightly less fear, but she was speaking of the same *he* Pet was terrified of. "Even if one of them was willing to help us, I'm not sure they could,"

Jay replied. "Rikai said Xeke was violent, with an insatiable need to feed, and he's a *good* guy. I don't want to know what—"

"He's not human?" Brina broke in. "Like me?" Before Jay could respond, she said, "Then the trainers aren't human. Or Jeshickah. It's just *me*?" She had barely been able to manage them when she was a vampire, with Daryl breathing down the neck of anyone who dared offend her, and Kaleo defending her simply because she was *his*. Now she would have no such protection.

"Lovely world you lived in," Jay commented, unable to screen out Brina's anxiety about those whom she'd once called associates, if not friends.

"It *was* lovely," she retorted. "There were ugly parts to it, but the same can be said of any civilization, even today."

"I don't think enslaving and torturing helpless humans, shapeshifters, and witches compares to anything we have today."

Many times in his life, Jay had been stared at by someone thinking, *Are you really this dense?* This might have been the worst, since it was coming from a woman famous for being so oblivious that she starved her slaves when she lost track of time.

"You live comfortably in one of the wealthiest nations in the world," Brina said, voice clipped. "You live on the bones of your own ancestors, who were eradicated by the expanding white populations. The food you eat, the clothes you wear, and the toys you buy are often made across the oceans by nameless, faceless workers living in conditions you would find intolerable."

"I try . . ."

Her glare silenced him.

"For years I was one of the poor, starving on the streets," she said flatly. "Then I was offered a chance to be immortal, and a lady. If you have never needed to sell your body just to get out of the rain for an hour, do not think to judge me—*or my brother*—for what we chose."

But you . . . and they . . . and we don't . . . No words came. Jay liked to think that no matter how bad things got, he would never turn into the kind of vicious creature Daryl had been. But he couldn't say for sure that he would have made a choice different from Brina's, which had been to take the good and ignore the rest.

He said the only honest thing he could think to say. "I am sorry you had to go through such hardship."

Unfortunately, he knew instantly that Brina had taken his words as more of the same mocking she had often received in her life. She bristled, and snapped, "The Shantel elemental may be justified in killing us all, but I for one intend to put my survival first, regardless. Are we in accord on that point?"

"I don't agree that she is justified in killing *my* family," Jay answered. "But I do agree that we need to stop her. The best idea I have is to talk to a parabiologist here at SingleEarth," he added, thinking of the video he had seen at Xeke's apartment. "She talked about elementals fighting back when the serpiente were made. If she's not sick, she might be able to help us."

⌘

Jay quashed a twinge of guilt as he refused Brina's request to come with him to the library, where a brief search of the archaeology and anthology sections revealed the name of the researcher Jay had recalled. He returned to Brina's quarantine room as soon as he had tracked down the woman's phone number, and then he put the conversation on speakerphone.

They quickly discovered that archaeologist Paula Epsilon was human, and had been sequestered in her office, unaware of any problems at SingleEarth, while she revised her next paper. Jay and Brina huddled around the phone as they both described the events of recent days in halting phrases.

"My god," Paula whispered for perhaps the hundredth time as Jay wrapped up.

"So, we need advice on handling an elemental," Jay said. "Do you know anything?"

"My god." Jay and Brina exchanged a frustrated glance as the human went silent for several seconds. "I mean, I wrote my dissertation on elementals and their influence on history," Paula said, "so I *know* plenty, but academic knowledge isn't going to help you much. You need a sorcerer, at the least, to have any chance of controlling an elemental."

"Great!" Jay said, latching on to the suggestion. "Do you know any?"

"A few. They tend to be pretty cranky," Paula said. "What I don't understand is how this other elemental can possibly be strong enough to even spit at Leona. I mean, when people say humanity discovered fire, they mean we discovered Leona. The

Epsilon theory states that Leona is directly responsible for the sudden shift in our evolutionary development, for our starting to use tools and—"

"And yet the Shantel elemental is challenging her," Jay interrupted, thinking, *She named a theory after herself. That's special.*

"The Shantel elemental is an earth elemental," Paula said, "and your friend said the Shantel protected a certain area of land, right? She is probably still bound to that land. You might find answers there."

"If we can get a sorcerer to help us, can you find Shantel territory?" Jay asked Brina.

"I think so." Turning back to the phone, Brina asked, "Do you know why she made me human?" Jay had heard the desperate question in Brina's mind since the start of the conversation. "Why would she protect me?"

"She didn't protect you. Humans are mortal," Paula answered. "Elementals *aren't*. A mortal life span is nothing to a creature who will exist as long as time itself. Given the vindictive nature of this particular elemental, I might theorize that she didn't kill you outright because she wanted you to see what she would do."

I will give you time, the elemental had said.

Time to watch everyone else die?

Before getting off the phone, Paula gave them contact information for a handful of sorcerers she knew, but it didn't make a difference; none of them was willing or able to come to the phone. Jay had just hung up from a short and frustrating conversation with some assistant named Cooper, when Jeremy knocked on the door.

"He's okay," Jay said to Brina, before he had even finished processing her thoughts to Jeremy, which was intense, to say the least.

"I'm sorry about before," Jeremy said, "but I didn't know what kind of danger you could be in, or could put other people in. You don't seem to have any symptoms, but as a precaution I've prescribed you a course of antibiotics. You got the first dose intravenously while you were out. I would like you to stay in isolation at least another day, though."

"You *attacked* and *drugged* me."

"I wasn't thinking clearly enough to be tactful," Jeremy said. "I was scared." *I'm still scared.* "How are you feeling?"

"We're both fine," Jay said, cutting off another angry reply from Brina. He knew why she was so scared. He had her memories of being under medieval quarantine, locked in a house to die. He also knew Jeremy probably hadn't had any choice. "How is Caryn?"

"Stable," Jeremy answered. "What you did helped a lot. How are *you* feeling?"

It would be an overstatement to say Jay was feeling *well,* after everything that had happened, but he wasn't sick. "I . . . think I may be immune." The Shantel elemental might have made Brina mortal as punishment, but it had seemed sincere in its offer to protect Jay.

"Then we need you out here," Jeremy said bluntly. "We're doing all we can with human medicine, and we're transferring the more advanced cases to hospitals outside SingleEarth as fast as we can, but we could use a witch."

"He isn't available," Brina barked.

"With all due respect, my *lady*," Jeremy said, as his last thread of patience snapped, "some of us have responsibilities beyond catering to you. The kitchen staff is preparing a meal for you, but that's as much time as we can devote to the apparently healthy right now."

Jay watched them without comment. What could he say? Jeremy was right. Brina was also right. Jay was one of the only people with a prayer of fixing what he had done . . . but *all* he had was a prayer, and a list of sorcerers who refused to come to the phone. Would he be more useful helping the sick?

"We left messages for everyone Paula suggested," Jay said to Brina. "Maybe someone will call us back. In the meantime, I should try to do some good here."

"Don't exhaust yourself, witch," Brina cautioned him. "You are too valuable to waste."

"I'm not comfortable with your concept of 'value,'" he replied, his mind on Midnight. He tossed his phone to Brina, who let it fall to the bed. "If any of our sorcerer friends call back, you can come get me. If we don't hear from anyone in, let's say an hour, we'll try something different."

An hour would be enough time for him to see what, if anything, he could do for the sick. It would also be more than enough time for him to think about every other option they had, which was, let's see . . . *nothing.*

Jay had never been good at intentionally shielding against

emotion and other empathic impressions. He had no idea how much he had instinctively screened out, until he walked into the gym-turned-sick-ward and felt the weight of emotion pressing on him. His stomach turned—or was that someone else's sensation? The air was thick and cloying, rank with chemicals, sweat, and despair. Percussive coughs broke through the constant rattle of pneumonic breathing.

"Jay," Jeremy asked, "where do you want to start? Does it make more sense to start with the sickest, or to work with those who aren't as far gone, so they don't reach that point, and then we can devote more medical resources to the critical cases? You know your power's limits better than I do."

My limits . . . I'm going to be sick.

Jay leaned back against the cold wall, closed his eyes, and drew his knife, seeking the *thrum* of ancestral magic and the comfort and focus it always brought.

He dropped the knife with a yelp as, instead of providing a peaceful pulse of soothing magic, it spiked him with a shock of raw power, as if he had put his hand in an electric outlet. The blade narrowly missed his foot, but all he could do was stare as the weight of a hundred sick and frightened minds crashed past his defenses.

—going to die here.
Never told her that—
—wonder if he will ever—
Who will take care of them when—
What did I do to deserve this?
"Jay?" *What happened to him?*

I need to get out of here.

Jay wasn't sure if that last thought was his or not, but it sounded good. Blindly, he shouldered Jeremy and at least one other solicitous body out of the way as he raced toward the front door. He stumbled out into drifting snow, dry-heaving as his stomach tried to give up what little food he had eaten too long ago.

He lay in the snow, feeling it soak through his clothes as he tried to just be still and—

"Go away!" he shouted at Jeremy when that anxious mind drew near. "I can't help you." *I can't help anyone. I'd just screw up even more.*

I told you not to go in there, Lynx chastised him from farther off in the woods. *Do you need me?*

I don't know what I need.

He wasn't the only one feeling hopeless. "It is not our responsibility to risk our lives for a fool's errand," a voice was saying. "We have the resources to keep our own people safe. We should be focused on that."

Jay could hear the words but couldn't feel the mind behind them. That should have told him who was speaking even before Xeke's voice responded.

"That has always been the big difference between you and me, Rikai," he said, the exasperation in his voice sufficient to make it clear that they had been arguing for a while. "I've never been willing to give up on the entire planet just because they're not my people. You— Jay? Is that you?"

Well, at least I didn't actually throw up in front of him, Jay thought. He was about to tell the vampire to go to hell anyway, because he didn't relish the idea of being miserable in front of him, when he processed what Xeke was saying. He was trying to convince Rikai to help.

Maybe they did still have a snow angel's chance in hell to fix this thing.

CHAPTER 21

"IT SEEMS I overestimated Xeke's instinct for survival," Rikai explained as she reached a hand down and unceremoniously yanked Jay to his feet. "So we're back."

You don't sound bitter about that at all, Jay thought, though he held his tongue. They needed Rikai's help, grudging or not.

"You look good," Jay remarked, looking between the two of them. Rikai's visible scars were gone, and the strength she had demonstrated helping him up was well beyond what she could have managed earlier. Xeke was a little flushed but clear-eyed.

"Thanks," Xeke answered. "You look like crap."

The vampire reached around Jay to brush snow off his back, which put him close enough to kiss—or bite, which was why

Jay tensed, recalling what Rikai had said about Xeke waking up starving.

"Has Brina won you from me already?" Xeke teased, noticing the withdrawal.

"What?" Jay knew perfectly well that Xeke was a flirt by nature. He shouldn't take it personally. So why did the vampire have this ability to tongue-tie him? "No, I just—Rikai seemed to think you were in rough shape. Are you okay?"

Xeke kissed Jay's cheek before stepping back. "Rikai did some kind of magical rewiring," he answered. "I don't understand it, but I feel pretty good."

"Whenever vampires feed, they give power to Leona," Rikai explained. "Their current madness is the result of her needing strength for battle. Thankfully, one of Xeke's progenitors has a bond to an earth elemental called Leshan." Rikai shrugged, as if this were perfectly normal, and common knowledge. "I was able to partially block Xeke's connection to Leona and tighten his bond to Leshan, which should protect him from the worst of the fallout."

"What's with the *L* names, anyway?" Xeke asked, apparently uninterested in the magical mechanics of his salvation. "Leona, Leshan, LeCoire; most of the elementals I know have *L* names."

"An elemental's true name is closely guarded," Rikai answered. "*Wise* sorcerers," she said, with a sharp glance at Jay, "may spend decades, perhaps even generations, trying to divine the true name of an elemental before ever speaking to or summoning it, since that name will give a mortal power over the immortal. The names we use are as real as an Internet messaging handle. The prefix *le* means 'a power or impetus,' in the ancient language," Rikai answered, "which is the language used among the elementals." Still focused on Jay, she added, "Idiot would-be sorcerers, on the other hand, meddle without any preparation or understanding of the powers with which they are playing, and cause things like *this*."

Jay was still flinching from the heat in her gaze when Xeke broke in.

"Yes, yes, I've heard the 'idiot would-be sorcerers' speech a hundred times today alone. Someone who becomes a vampire hunter either has an irresistible urge to murder people or an irresistible urge to get killed protecting strangers. Blaming them for poorly planned, suicidal stunts in the line of duty is like blaming a cat for jumping after that stupid red dot."

"Thank you, Xeke, for that very flattering defense," Jay said. "So the short story is, you two are safe for now?"

"Yes," Rikai answered. "As are you. Currently, the Shantel elemental has tied itself to you, and severed your bond to Leona. If Shantel wins, you keep that bond. If Leona wins, she will surely take you back like a prize of war. You will be fine. So *please* convince this fool friend of mine that we do not need to risk our lives trying to fight the immortals."

Jay glanced at Xeke, who raised a brow, thinking to Jay, *Fish gotta swim, birds gotta fly, hunters gotta hunt. You won't walk away from this.*

"Someone told us that, if we had a sorcerer to help and

could get to Shantel territory, we might be able to do something there," Jay said. "Brina is inside, and she knows where Shantel land was."

Reluctantly, Rikai nodded. "That would be the best place to make a stand, yes. It would put us inside the strongest of the elemental's defenses."

They had a plan. It was crazy, but it was a plan. Step one was going to Shantel land, which was apparently a good distance away. Rikai seemed to think that once they were inside Shantel territory, they would have some leverage over the elemental. Step two would be summoning the elemental and then, as far as Jay could tell, completely winging the next phase and hoping they could find a way to control a creature with godlike power and a whole lot of wrath. That part relied on Rikai, so it was okay that Jay didn't understand it all.

"We should fly," Brina said with a trill of excitement, as she pointed to their destination on a map. Planes had not existed when she was mortal, and as a vampire, she had never needed one.

"We'll need equipment to travel in the snow," Jay added, in response to Brina's mental images of the area.

"I'll talk to my people and get the jet ready," Xeke said. He pulled out his wallet and opened it to retrieve an outrageously shiny silver card, which he held out to Jay. "Do you think you can put together everything we'll need?"

Jay took the credit card with a kind of reverence. He received a small allowance from his family, but he wasn't the type to maintain credit.

"I might not be able to get to all the stores we need before they close," he answered, compiling a list in his head, and realizing it was already nearly dark again. "But I'll manage."

Rikai let out a long, exasperated sigh before saying, "If we are going to fly across the country to fight elementals, I will need additional supplies."

"I will go with Jay," Brina announced. She glanced down at her long gown, thinking, *This is not at all ideal for a winter wonderland adventure.*

Without intending to, Jay found himself humming a bar of the song "Winter Wonderland," which made Brina laugh, which in turn made Xeke and Rikai stare at them both as if they were lunatics.

"We'll meet at the airport," Xeke said. "Remember, we're all on borrowed time."

Brina handled being waited on by staff excited to help them better than Jay did. While Jay grabbed the basics—topping a thousand dollars before he had even finished choosing a tent and backpacks—Brina gathered suggestions on food and clothing. At least a dozen times, he heard her bell-like laugh before she assured worried store employees, "*He* knows what he's doing."

"Don't worry. We've got a friend who's an expert," Jay kept assuring the friendly staff who buzzed around them, concerned that Jay and Brina were embarking on a deep-woods winter backpacking trip with next to no experience, as evidenced by their total lack of gear.

Jay had backpacked before, even in the deepest winter, but between his magic and his connection to Lynx, he had always been able to go minimalist. In a pinch, Jay could sleep in a snowdrift and be fine. None of his backpacking equipment was relevant to what they were embarking on now.

Disgusting stuff, Brina thought as she gamely chose polyester undergarments and jackets designed to keep a human body warmer than natural fibers would. *Vile texture. No wonder humans get so cranky.*

The adventure continued at the next store, which had been closed for an hour. Jay broke in through a back door, hoping there wasn't an automatic alarm and that—if any of them lived through this—SingleEarth could deal with any legal repercussions relating to the blinking security cameras.

Brina followed with a quiver of excitement. She helped grab additional fuel, food, and the last odds and ends the first store hadn't had in stock. They didn't dare stay long, in case police *were* coming.

Satisfied that they had done the best they could with limited time, an apparently unlimited budget, and a desire not to go to jail, they squeezed into the over-full car and sped away to the rendezvous point. Lynx curled up on Brina's lap, oblivious to the passengers' rapid conversation, as Brina asked question after question about how humans traveled and survived in such conditions.

Jay spent most of the three-hour ride in Xeke's private jet opening packages and compulsively packing and repacking backpacks. No matter what other equipment they brought, he felt naked without his Marinitch blade. His magic might still feel the same to *him*, but whatever the Shantel elemental had done to him, it had made his own knife violently reject him. No amount of butane fuel, freeze-dried food, warm clothes, or high-tech gadgets would make him feel good about the lack of his blade.

As they transferred from the jet to a rented Jeep, Jay continued working on the problem of how to lug all their gear with them. Jay could carry a heavy backpack over a long distance, but Brina probably couldn't. Xeke lifted his for the first time and immediately said, "I can take more," while Rikai attempted to lift hers and then shook her head. She wasn't as crippled as before, but her strength was even more limited than a human's.

Jay was still fiddling with the packs as they reached the edge of the proverbial deep dark forest. They had been able to drive as far as a campground, with trails leading into one of the largest national forests. After those paths ended, they would have to blaze their own trail through the evergreen trees.

"At least it's not a stormy night," Jay remarked as he stepped down from the Jeep, earning a glare from Rikai, a quirked brow from Xeke, and a chuckle from Brina. Lynx leapt out of Brina's lap, his senses on full alert.

In fact, it was an overcast and chill dawn. The ground held a few inches of snow, crusted with ice in many places. They had brought snowshoes, but Jay hoped they wouldn't be needed, since he was the only one with any experience using them.

Check it out? Jay asked Lynx as he arranged their supplies on a modified sled known as a pulk. The cat ran off to scout, and Jay kept packing. Given that they had no firm idea of how long they would need to travel, he had brought as much food and fuel as they could possibly transport. He hoped the snow would stay thick enough for the sled to slide smoothly.

"Do you need help?" Xeke asked, startling Jay from his contemplation of weight and balance.

"How's this?" he asked, offering Xeke the repacked backpack, which was now significantly heavier than a human would be able to carry for any length of time.

The vampire tested the pack, and then nodded.

Want rabbit for dinner? Lynx asked as he returned. *That or chipmunk. Also smells of deer and coyote.*

Let me know if you scent anything else, Jay said. *Especially anything big enough to eat us.*

He had almost finished setting up the pulk, when he was startled by another thought, just as clear as Lynx's but from an entirely different mind.

See the way the branches sparkle where they're encased in ice, Brina thought to him.

To both of them, Jay realized only when Lynx replied, *Slippery to walk on. And sometimes it drops on your head when you sleep.*

Brina looked around, as if almost aware of Lynx's reply but unable to place the sound.

"It is lovely," Jay agreed.

"I could do a beautiful portrait of the lynx," Brina remarked. Did she realize she hadn't started the conversation out loud?

She talks like you do, Lynx replied to Jay's contemplation. *Half in voice-yips, half in mind. And she expects people to hear both, just like you do.*

Was that the result of having been telepathic for years, as a vampire? Or just another one of Brina's quirks?

"We should get going," Rikai said, staring at the mouth of the path with frustration. After the second time Jay had repacked her bag, she had taken half the items out to accommodate her ritual paraphernalia.

Jay glanced down at the clunky watchlike GPS thing he never would have touched if he had been spending his own money or wandering familiar forests. Xeke had given the device coordinates based on Brina's best guess as she'd looked at a series of maps, and it currently claimed that their destination was about thirty-five miles to the northeast. With fair weather, good trails, and experienced hikers, that distance could easily be traveled in a couple days, but Jay doubted they would have any of those luxuries.

They didn't even have a straight path to their destination. Instead, they headed first to the base of the original Midnight, from which Brina believed it was only a short journey to Shantel territory—assuming that her estimate of Midnight's location was correct, that they could find Midnight without getting trapped in its magical gravity well, and that the magic in the Shantel land didn't throw them back out.

Rikai believed that the Shantel power would draw them in, because Jay and Brina were now bonded to it, but even she admitted that was just a theory.

Yes, if all went well, they should be able to confront a homicidal immortal very soon.

CHAPTER 22

JAY BECAME INCREASINGLY grateful for Brina's odd conversational style as they began their hike. The more out of breath Brina became, the more she communicated in mental images instead of speaking aloud, and the clearer it became why she was an artist. A simple s'mores granola bar triggered a deep, meditative analysis of the various tastes and textures.

Her mental energy gave him hope. Her joy at the way the sun sparkled on the snow made the impressions he received from Rikai and Xeke easier to bear.

The comfort Xeke had experienced as a result of Rikai's work was now fading, and was being replaced by hunger and restlessness. Her rewiring made it possible for him to keep control, but he couldn't ignore the spicy heat of the witch's blood, or the coppery tang of Brina's human blood, or even the syrupy sweet lure of Rikai's blood—though the last would be poison to him.

Rikai was still shielding her mind, but Jay suspected she was keeping pace with the rest of them out of sheer stubbornness. The only thought she let slip through to him was that she considered Brina's presence a boon because she could be used as a human sacrifice. She expected him to be reasonable if it came to that.

Jay chose not to comment.

Unlike the woods behind Xeke's and Kendra's homes, this forest was vast, teeming with the life one would expect in untouched wilderness. As the group moved farther away from human civilization, Lynx pointed out territorial markers left behind by cougars, bobcats, and other lynxes. He caught a snowshoe rabbit, and lorded it over the rest of them that he had hot, fresh meat while they settled in for a night of dried, packaged foods.

The tent was snug with the four of them, even though Rikai sat cross-legged in a trance instead of sleeping, and Jay had decided that it would take less energy to keep people warm with his power than it would to lug bulky subzero sleeping bags.

That logic had seemed sound, right up until the moment when he had Xeke spooned against his back, Brina snuggled against his chest, and Lynx keeping his feet warm. He had been worried that Brina's ladylike manners might make her balk at the sleeping arrangements, but she accepted them as part of the ongoing quest.

Jay was the one who had some qualms, mostly about the vampire nuzzling at his neck and not-so-idly recalling their first conversation.

Was it was safer to give a little blood and risk being weaker in the morning, or to leave the vampire hungry? *This is only the first night. What about tomorrow?*

"Fire is bound in blood, but earth is bound in flesh," Rikai said, making Jay jump. "I can't entirely block the blood-hunger, because that comes from Leona's seeking power, but all he needs to be able to sustain himself is to be able to touch you, as he is now." That was . . . unsettling. Rikai added, "He should not be able to draw enough power from you to be a danger, but I will keep watch just in case."

And you care so much about my well-being. Rikai kept Jay with them for the same reason she tolerated Brina: she thought he would be useful. Knowing that wasn't the same as actually trusting her.

A restless night led into an even longer day in which their off-trail hike became increasingly challenging. Jay's irritation only grew as his foot skidded on an ice-slicked rock and he fell into a winter-stripped thornbush.

As he extracted himself, he felt a burst of triumph from Brina. Throwing herself down to look more closely at the bush, she exclaimed, "Look!"

She frowned up at them all when they failed to respond, and then touched a reddish bulb growing at the end of one branch. "Rose hips," she said, as if that should have been sufficient explanation.

"Are you craving tea?" Rikai snapped. Rose hips were the fruit left behind after a rose's blooms fell.

Brina stood up and announced, with what sounded like genuine disappointment, "It took Rhok nearly a century to breed a rose that blooms so dark it appears black to human eyes, and you look at it like it's a dead bush."

"It isn't blooming at the moment," Xeke pointed out.

"And it hasn't been eaten," Jay replied as he examined the bush more closely. Long-stemmed formal roses generally couldn't survive in darkly canopied forests. This one not only had, but the rose's fruit hadn't been touched by any of the numerous animals who should have enjoyed it as a delicious snack.

"Silver's line is the one known for black roses," Xeke said.

"When Silver's line took over after Midnight's fall, they made the symbol their own," Brina replied. "I know this place. See these stones, here, and here?" It took a great deal of imagination to see anything more than random rocks strewn amidst trees and brush, but Brina recognized something, and through her Jay could see the plaza that had once been in that place.

"This was a freeblood market," Brina said, one gloved hand lingering on a stone with faint vestiges of etched letters, its message long lost to lichen and moss. "All the shapeshifter nations traded their best goods here. We should be less than a day from Midnight proper." With a slight pout, she added, "There used to be a road."

"Well, there's no road now," Jay replied, more sharply than he'd intended. He glanced down at the stupid GPS, which informed him that they had overshot their destination . . . suggesting that the coordinates they were using hadn't been correct in the first place.

"Let's try that path," Xeke suggested, pointing.

"That's a deer trail," Rikai replied.

Jay turned toward the unremarkable break in the woods. He wouldn't have noticed it if the vampire hadn't pointed it out first, and it still didn't seem a likely prospect. It wasn't even going in the right direction.

Lynx gave him a mental poke, saying, *You don't know where you are or where you're going. How can a direction be wrong?*

Pondering that insight, Jay stepped closer, and realized the path was wider than he had first thought. The closer he moved to it, the more he realized his eyes were playing tricks on him. This *wasn't* a deer trail.

"I think we've found your road," Jay said to Brina. "Xeke, I'm going to need you to tell me if you see forks . . . or anything dangerous, come to think of it. I don't think it's a coincidence that you saw this and I didn't."

"Where—" Rikai paused, closed her eyes, and tilted her head as if listening. At last she said, "The spells here are old but still powerful. And very discreet, designed not to be noticed even by a witch."

Especially a witch who normally carries a hunter's blade, I'd bet, Jay thought, lamenting the loss of his usual weapon.

"Once we get to Midnight proper," Brina said as she led the way up the old road, "there is another path, traveling nearly due east, that should take us into Shantel land. Then it is simply a matter of—"

Blackness.

Pain.

Jay opened his eyes to find himself sprawled in the snow, with Brina kneeling next to him. Xeke looked concerned, but Rikai's face simply held contempt.

Flames, like the fires of hell. Flesh scalding—

"Guard your mind," Rikai suggested belatedly.

Jay turned his head, trying to see the mind he could feel so clearly. Brina gripped his hand, crushing his fingers, and he knew she saw it too: a semitransparent shape, almost humanoid, but—

"Ghosts, nothing more," Rikai said. "Unless you invite them into your brain, they are harmless."

What most people called ghosts were just impressions left behind by strong emotions. Jay had encountered them before, but never this powerfully. The pain this ghost was radiating was beyond Jay's comprehension. It made his bones ache as he forced himself to stand and keep moving.

The farther they traveled up the road, the thicker the impressions became.

When Jay was a boy, his history lessons had included stories of Midnight. As for its fall, that had been described in simple terms: on September 22, 1804, Midnight burned to the ground. No one knew who was responsible, though everyone had celebrated the destruction, which had been so complete that the slave trainers had not been able to gather their power fast enough to re-subjugate the witches and shapeshifters before they could raise arms to defend themselves.

Those lessons were made real in the early twilight as the forest spat them onto the carcass of what had once been an empire's terrible heart.

Nature should have taken over in the last two centuries, but it hadn't been allowed. Magic had salted the ground in this clearing, leaving it a dead zone inhabited by nothing more than what might have once been stone—now twisted and melted as if torn from a volcano—and the ghostly impressions of those who had once lived in this place. Sheets of ice, gritty and black from ash, ringed the area, but the ruins themselves glowed hot like coals under the darkening sky.

Jay could hear the memories wail in fury, and pain, and helplessness, and—more than anything else—confusion. *Why?* they asked.

Rikai crept close, even though that meant crawling on the ice, until she could hold her hands above the glistening coals and say in a voice that sounded half hypnotized, "They say every major power in the world was involved in bringing Midnight down. They poured their magic into this spot. I can feel them. . . ."

"Jay, I do not wish to camp here for the night," Brina said, her voice seeming oh-so-distant as Jay struggled not to hear the screams of the dead.

"Agreed," Xeke said.

Lynx hissed, and Jay realized that he couldn't hear his long-time companion over all the other voices pressing against him. Brina reached down and stroked Lynx between the ears, while looking up at Jay with concern.

"East, you said?" he asked her. Was he shouting?

She nodded, and caught his shoulders to physically turn him until his back was to the setting sun. They all wanted to get as far away as possible.

Almost all.

"Rikai?"

"Come here!" Rikai called, her voice breathy. "This is incredible. I think—"

Jay heard Xeke trying to reason with the Triste, but he didn't wait for her response. He needed to get away from this place. The others would have to catch up.

CHAPTER 23

THE MEMORY OF blood and fire pressed in around Brina as she ran from Midnight and every gruesome recollection the sight had brought to mind. She followed Jay, who led them at a frantic pace well past sunset, until clouds obscured any hint of stars or the nearly full moon and it was too dark to see one foot in front of the other.

Preparing food and setting up their camp in the inky black was challenging, as was trying to find enough privacy to take care of awkward human bodily functions without becoming totally lost. She was grateful that Lynx stayed near, sweetly compassionate in the way he called to her in the darkness when she strayed the wrong way.

Though they made camp late, they started early the next

morning. Brina struggled to keep up with Jay's pace, refusing to be the weak member of their party. Exequías and Rikai lumbered behind her, and she kept her eyes firmly on the wide-eyed witch. Eventually, it was Lynx who set teeth into Jay's calf with a snarl.

Jay jerked his head up as if from a trance, and looked around at his exhausted companions. "Sorry," he said. "I keep feeling . . ." He trailed off, and shivered. "I think it's the same magic that tried to hide the road from me."

"I'm no expert at magic," Exequías said, "but doesn't it take power to maintain something like this? What kind of spell is still this strong two hundred years later?"

"The kind of spells Midnight would buy," Rikai answered, shouldering past them at a slower but no less inexorable pace. The rest of them fell in line behind her, Jay's steps tense, as if he were still fighting the instinct to run. "They were first crafted through sacrifice. When Midnight was attacked, the spells were fed with slaughter, and enough magic to leave stone smoldering for centuries."

"You mean the spells got stronger after the attack?" Brina asked. She had no magical expertise personally, but she knew some of the witches who had supported Midnight. *Black* was not a dark enough word to describe some of their rituals.

"More than that," Rikai answered. "I think it's no coincidence that the civilizations who lent their power to this attack have all fallen into decline since. Before that attack, even Midnight feared the Shantel, the Azteka, and the shm'Ahnmik. They were *worth* fearing. Now they're so insignificant that many consider them myths. The wreckage their actions left behind has been like an open wound that any parasite could use. I doubt Midnight's defense spells were the only opportunistic leeches who noticed." With a glance back and an unsettling smile, she added, "I know that *I* certainly intend to return, once other matters are—"

She broke off, going still. Brina moved up beside her and realized what had made the witch stop: the road was gone.

Looking back revealed more of the same. Without warning, they were in the middle of pristine wilderness.

"How did we lose the path?" Jay asked, looking around.

"We must have crossed into Shantel territory," Brina replied. "There are no paths here." She had never traveled through Shantel land, but she had heard stories from others who had. Once within the forest's magical snare, no compass or map could save you.

"But we were just *on* a path," Jay protested.

"And now we're *not*," Rikai snapped. "The Shantel were masters of illusion. Jay, what do you sense?"

Jay closed his eyes. "Power," he answered. "It has a feline flavor. I can't sense where it's coming from."

"Let me see if I can pierce a hole in this veil," Rikai said, and she folded her legs to sit cross-legged on the ground. From her pack, she pulled what looked like a long silver chain. As she made a circle in the snow around her, the metal glowed so white-hot that Brina had to look away from its glare.

Brina paced a little, and opened a water bottle to take a few careful sips. Her throat was sore from panting as she'd struggled to keep up with Jay's near-run, and her legs felt stiff and tingly. If she sat down, she doubted she would be able to get back up quickly.

Unexpectedly, she met Jay's gaze. Something in those hazel eyes made her want to reach out to him, but before she could give into the impulse, Rikai stood up and announced confidently, "This way."

They continued, but less than an hour later, Lynx let out a frustrated yowl, and Jay said, "We've turned around."

"No, we haven't," Rikai replied.

"If we're heading east, the sun shouldn't be in front of us this time of day," Jay insisted. He paused to turn on the watch-like compass on his wrist, and then turned it off again with a sound of disgust.

Brina explained, "You can't trust the sun in the Shantel forest, any more than you can trust your gadgets."

"I trust my power," Rikai replied firmly.

Lynx growled, but what choice did they have? They followed Rikai. With sore legs and an increasingly aching head, Brina forced one foot in front of another, until, as the woods began to darken, Jay announced, "We've been here before."

"We haven't—"

"We *have*," the witch interrupted sharply. "Lynx can recognize his own scent markers. We've been here."

"You trust cat pee over magic?" Rikai asked incredulously.

"I do," Exequías broke in. "Cat pee never lies. And it's too dark to travel farther tonight. We'll have to come up with another plan in the morning."

Morning came far too soon.

"Brina?"

She mumbled a complaint in response to whoever was saying her name and touching her shoulder. Then her cheek, and her neck.

"Brina, can you hear me?"

She attempted to swat at the irritation, and found her wrist caught. Didn't they understand she was *tired*? Couldn't she sleep a little longer?

"Go away." Her voice cracked. Her throat hurt. Swallowing hurt more.

"She's sick?" Exequías asked.

She sat bolt upright, protesting, "Of course I'm not." But moving so quickly made her head spin and her stomach twist. She gagged, and that made her cough, and once she started, she couldn't seem to stop.

Oh, God, it hurts.

"Brina, calm down," Jay said. "You're hyperventilating."

He didn't know. He couldn't understand, no matter what his magic told him about her.

She wasn't sick.

She couldn't be sick.

She just needed some air.

She slapped hands away as they tried to keep her from pulling on her boots, and then she shoved her way out of the stifling tent. She fled the accusation of illness. She fled the memory of clutching Angelica's cooling body. She fled the nights of huddling in doorways, trying to get out of the rain and wondering if the rattling in her lungs was pneumonia, or tuberculosis . . . or plague. . . .

Once outside, however, the winter cold cut straight through her. She tucked her bare hands inside her fleece sleeves as she turned back toward the tent, trying to hold her head high as if she hadn't been panicking.

The campsite had vanished. Her footprints filled in as she watched, as if an unfelt wind were drifting the snow until there was no path to follow back.

"Hello?" she called.

Foolish, she thought. *The Shantel never liked our kind.*

But I'm not one of my kind anymore.

I'm talking to myself.

She tried to focus, but exhaustion coupled with fever to cloud her thoughts. Maybe if she took a nap, she would be able to think.

"No, stupid," she said. *Now I'm talking* out loud *to myself.* But she kept doing it, because thinking silently was harder. "You can't sleep in the snow. Humans don't wake up when they do that. Need to get back to camp. They'll look for me. Won't find me, if the Shantel magic doesn't want them to."

She started walking. She couldn't make a straight line. She drifted; she stumbled and occasionally bumped into trees. Her vision was blurry, and it seemed to take a monumental effort to lift each leg.

"Don't want to die," she said, over and over, until her throat hurt too much and she couldn't speak or swallow anymore.

"Brina!"

She turned, awash with gratitude. "Jay!"

He caught her up in his arms. Warmth seeped off him; she snuggled close.

"I tried to tell you before you ran off that I can help you," he said. "This isn't like before, Brina. You're a little sick, but it's probably just a cold, *maybe* the flu, but nothing I can't help with. You'll be okay, I promise."

His voice was comforting.

"Let's get you back to the tent," he said. "We should eat before . . ."

He trailed off, which made her glance up. He was looking around, obviously concerned.

"Xeke? Rikai?"

No reply.

"They were right here," Jay said. "Damn it. I didn't go that far. I didn't think we could be split up when we should still be close enough to *see* each other." He rested his cheek on her hair.

Brina yelped, startled, as a furry beast suddenly tumbled into sight. Lynx! He yowled, then turned about, took two steps, and glanced back at them with an impatient expression.

"He's found something," Jay said. "Let's go."

Brina was still a bit unsteady, but it was nice to walk without layers of clothes, the heavy pack weighing her down, and the sled snagging on rocks and brambles every few minutes.

Jay's hand was solid in hers, and his power wove a sphere of warmth around them. Her headache started to fade.

The feeling of unreality continued as they emerged from the forest and found a low stone wall, with deep drifting snow leading up to it but barely a dusting of powder on top or on the other side of the wall, as if the wind and trees and structures had colluded to prevent the snow from falling there. Jay placed one foot atop the wall, twisting to reach back to take her hand, and suddenly her fingers itched for a paintbrush.

A variation on Cernunnos, she decided, *the stag lord of the hunt.* Except, instead of a stag, Jay had his lynx companion. She hadn't had an image appeal to her so powerfully since . . . since the days before she had wept over her brother's dead body.

"If we survive, I'll happily model for you," her Cernunnos said, shaking his hair back. It billowed around his face, the sunset behind him bringing out all the gold and copper highlights in his deep auburn hair.

Maybe he wasn't Cernunnos. Maybe he was Dionysus, Greek god of revelry. In his many forms and stories, Dionysus—also known as Bacchus—was wild and free-spirited, but with a dark side. He taught mankind to make wine, but also caused the vicious dismemberment of a prince who'd dared insult him and question his godliness. He was often depicted with a leopard.

Jay grinned. "I like that one," he said.

It was nice, not needing to speak aloud to him. She could perform near-magic with oils, but even she could never perfectly create the images she saw in her head. The colors didn't exist, and canvas for all its versatility could still only capture a single, still moment. So limited.

She froze the image in her mind and then let him help her across the wall.

Inside the courtyard, it was warm, and bright with dappled springlike light. The magic was still alive and breathing, willful.

She drew a breath, coughed once, lightly, but then completed the breath, laughed, and tossed her hair back from her face. If Jay was Dionysus, who was she? Not some little lost girl. No. Never again. Maybe Artemis, goddess of the hunt?

I could be Artemis.

Jay smiled at her again, a beautiful, feral expression, and said, "If I have a goddess at my side, how hard can it possibly be to conquer an elemental? C'mon, let's hunt."

It was false bravado, and yet it wasn't. They both knew the next moment could be their last, that if they had really lost the others, they had no way to fight and no plan to move forward. But that was later. This was *now,* and right now was an instant of pure beauty.

CHAPTER 24

THE SHANTEL LAND was neither empty nor lifeless. The wood buildings were centuries old and crumbling, roofs collapsed inside and taken by rot and woodland creatures, but the forest had not overgrown these open spaces the way it should have. Though Jay's eyes revealed no shapeshifters prowling through the clearings, he did not feel alone. Echoes of power and personalities lingered—trapped by Shantel magic?

No animal smells, Lynx said, *or marks.*

Brina edged closer to both of them. This felt like a haunted place to her, and even if it was not malevolent, that didn't mean it had their best interests at heart.

"What happened to the shapeshifters who lived here?" Jay asked. "Could they not survive after losing the *sakkri*?"

"I do not think they would have sold the *sakkri* if they could not survive without her," Brina reasoned, "but the Shantel may not have been able to survive after losing Midnight. It was a hard time."

"Hard for the vampires, I'm sure," Jay replied, his mind distracted by trying to make out the currents of thought and power around him. He kept thinking he saw the sleek movements of hunting cats out of the corner of his eye, but turning made the illusions disappear. "The less-fortunate species rejoiced."

Something glittered in the dirt, and Brina knelt to pick it up as she said, "They rejoiced in their freedom, but freedom and comfort rarely go hand in hand. Do you think Midnight was nothing more than an empire of slaves?" The item she had found turned out to be a silver pacifier, which she stared at for several moments, unable to avoid picturing little Angelica.

"Do you want to talk about her?" Jay asked.

Not yet, she thought. She had loved that child, the first infant she had ever held.

"This area is rich in silver these days, but in Midnight's time there were no mines here. Where do you think this silver came from? For that matter, where did your ancestors get the silver for their hunters' blades?"

"Wherever people got silver two hundred years ago," Jay answered. The question wasn't idle, obviously, though Brina's thoughts were still too tangled in the image of Angelica's blackening face and wheezing cough for Jay to get her point without asking, "I don't know. Where?"

"Zacatecas, Potosí," Brina answered. "Modern Mexico, Bolivia, even Peru. This silver traveled at least two thousand miles before it reached this spot, in a day when there were no planes or trains. Maybe it went to the avian shapeshifters first, since they are famous for their silverwork. They sold it to some Shantel mother, probably in exchange for furs or leather. And do you know where those trades would have taken place?" In her mind, Jay again saw the market they had found. "In an age when few humans traveled a hundred miles from their homes, Midnight had minds that remembered the great empires of the Aztecs, the Romans, and the Chinese. We maintained trade routes that humans wouldn't discover for centuries. Your kind might not have openly purchased Midnight's tainted goods, but I guarantee that you prospered from it even while you tried to kill us."

"Prospered?" Jay snapped. "Most of us were wiped out!"

"And those who were not founded SingleEarth. You have your own empire now to control humans, and the shapeshifter kings who once bowed to us now bow to you."

"We founded SingleEarth for protection, not to rule."

"Why do you think Mistress Jeshickah founded Midnight?" Brina challenged. "The Inquisition killed dozens of those who thought they were immortal. Shapeshifter mercenaries helped." She looked at his expression, and her shoulders squared defensively. "I am not saying this makes Midnight good or Single-Earth evil. But I know the modern Midnight fears SingleEarth. Don't you think that should concern you?"

"I trust my kin."

Brina smiled sadly. "And apparently you trust that your kin will always be in charge of a massive international organization that has its fingers in the governments and economies of every major civilization in the modern world. That makes it an empire—one with a branch devoted to mercenary work, if rumors of an alliance with the Bruja guilds are to be believed."

"Okay, I'll admit there is a *potential* for abuse, but that's different from an empire totally devoted to slavery and subjugation."

"I believe in two absolute laws of politics," Brina admitted. "Power corrupts, and good intentions are the fastest way to hell. Oh, and none of us really wants to live on our own. That's why we make these alliances in the first place. There's no shame in not wanting to be alone."

What had happened to the addled woman so known for obliviousness that Xeke had been surprised she had noticed her own brother's death?

As Brina flinched instinctively from Jay's hard stare, he learned the answer to his question: no one had ever listened to her before, or challenged her when she'd spoken up, no matter how outrageous she'd gotten. She was enjoying arguing with him.

As the uncomfortable moment stretched, Brina dropped the silver pacifier and said, "All I see here are cracked plaza tiles, collapsed buildings, and an ancient stone wall. What are we hoping to *do*?"

Jay wanted to prod her back into the fight, both because

he wanted to come up with a retort to defend SingleEarth and because she was entertaining to wrangle with.

There will be time for that if we can figure out how to save the world.

"I don't know," Jay admitted. "I had thought maybe we could reason with the elemental, but if it knows we're here, it's ignoring us. We need Rikai and Xeke."

"What I know of Shantel magic is that you could not step a foot in their forest without the *sakkri* knowing. The *sakkri* controls the magic, and it controls where you go," Brina said. "Right now, you're the only witch this woods has. Bring Rikai and Xeke here."

It was on the tip of Jay's tongue to point out that a Marinitch empath and a Shantel *sakkri* were very different, but maybe it wasn't as crazy as it seemed. Jay *had* been able to mingle with the woods around the new Midnight, even though that magic had been outright hostile toward him. The Shantel elemental had tried to help him the last time he'd communicated with it. If this forest considered him an ally, maybe he *could* speak to it, albeit in his own way.

"I'll try," he said, earning another sunlight smile from her. "I'll probably space out while I do this. Touch me if you need my attention, okay?"

Brina nodded.

Jay sat on the ground, where he could put his bare hands against the cobblestone ground, then closed his eyes. Beneath the cobbles was raw earth. Through that earth, he stretched his awareness as far as he could, not looking for animal minds but drifting in the ebb and flow of the power around him.

Impressive. The magic wrapped into this land was so complex, it dazzled him. He envisioned it like a spiderweb, with crystal drops of mist stuck to it. Each bead of moisture was a living being, hanging on the gossamer strands.

Except spiderwebs were fragile. This had existed, and would continue, for ages.

Brina was a bright glow near him. Yes, her vampirism was gone, but he realized she had power in her, like a witch's magic, lingering, dormant in her blood. Could that power wake?

He skipped his awareness along the line of Shantel territory, through the leaves and winter breezes, the pine trees stretching in the cold air, and the deciduous trees tranquil in their long sleep.

He reached for Brina's hand. She hesitated before taking his, concerned that he had told her to touch him only if she needed to interrupt him, but then followed his lead.

Look.

It was clumsy, like a child's first steps, but once she realized what he was trying to do, she worked with him. Her artist's mind was able to manipulate the patterns of magic in an instinctive way, so she was able to "see" as he did. The trees were his nerves, and the animals, his eyes. He could feel the power like a heartbeat and a pulse, a thought that made Brina nervous, until she recklessly submerged herself in the forest's awareness.

They both could have drowned that way, forgetting their purpose in the lazy pulse of the forest's slow life, but then they touched Rikai and Xeke. Those unwelcome powers were an irritation, like hot ash falling on the skin. Both of them were in pain, exhausted and starving, not for food but for *power* . . . and for hope. They had been lost since Jay and Brina had disappeared.

This way, Jay called.

Brina echoed him, lending her power to his. *This way,* she said. *Hurry.*

Together, they siphoned some of the forest's abundant energy into the Triste and vampire, giving them the strength to stand and walk.

Once Rikai and Xeke drew near, though, their efforts drew the elemental's attention. Until then the forest had responded to Jay and Brina, but now the elemental itself noticed what they were doing. As Rikai and Xeke hoisted themselves over the stone borders of the plaza and hurried to Jay and Brina, the spiderweb of magic shook itself, flinging Jay and Brina away.

When they opened their eyes, disoriented, a figure loomed in front of them.

She did not register to any sense but Jay's eyes; to his magic, she was an extension of the land itself, in no way a separate being. Once, this body had belonged to a shapeshifter with ink-black skin and hair marked with white. Now, it had been claimed by darkness itself.

True darkness wasn't evil. It was the ultimate neutral. People could kill each other under its cover, or make love. Like so many things, the only value the darkness held was that which others gave it, often based on its use—or ancient fears, of course,

since so many things had used the darkness for their own ne-
farious purposes.

This darkness might once have been the neutral coolness of
a deep cave, beyond the interference of fire's light, but now it
had been tainted by pain and loss and anger. It looked at Jay,
and in its face he saw the fury of betrayal.

CHAPTER 25

THE CREATURE THAT stood before them, possessing the shapeshifter's form, no longer saw Jay as an ally.

"Shantel," Rikai said, stepping between Jay and the hostile immortal, "I know now how you have grown so strong. All that power in the ruins of Midnight, all the *flesh* sacrificed that day—you used them to bond yourself to everyone at the battle, including the other elementals. Since that day, you have secretly fed on every elemental that gave magic to that fight. That is how you are now strong enough to challenge Leona, while others have faded into obscurity."

Jay would have been happy to let the Triste negotiate with the elemental, but Brina stepped forward, madly, and reached for the once-shapeshifter's hand. As in everything, she saw heartbreaking beauty in this figure.

She is the night, Brina thought.

That's not your Pet anymore, Jay thought back. The elemental was clearly occupying the shapeshifter's body, but Jay doubted that made it weaker. *Maybe you shouldn't move so—*

Brina touched the elemental's arm, and the jolt of power passed through her and Jay both, blinding and deafening them for several moments.

By the time he recovered, the world around him had changed. The shadowy felines that had haunted the corners of his perception before were now solid and visible before him. Cats of all colors and patterns—many not found in nature—stalked around them. They were not entirely real, but neither could they be disregarded.

It took him three tries to see Lynx, who looked pale and colorless against the visions. Lynx backed away from the other cats, bristling.

The elemental stood above them like a vengeful angel.

"We didn't come here to hurt you or any of your . . . people," Jay said as he pushed himself slowly back to his feet. "We came here to try to ask you not to hurt my people. They never harmed you or any of your—"

"They did not help us, either," the elemental replied, its voice heavy like thunder. Jay feared that its words alone might have the power to destroy him. Listening to it speak made his bones ache.

"Who do you think destroyed Midnight centuries ago?" Jay argued. Where were Xeke and Rikai? Nearby, he hoped. . . .

"What good did that little revolution do, when the worst creatures all survived? When, after your kin declared victory, my child continued to live in suffering?"

You're reasoning with it the wrong way, Brina thought.

"Spirit of the Shantel," Brina said, her voice gentle and respectful, "you wear the form of one who used to belong to me."

The elemental snarled, recoiling. *"The sakkri of the Shantel belongs to no one!"*

Brina tilted her head, as if confused. "I know of no *sakkri.* I know only of a creature named Pet. Has she not introduced herself to you as such?"

Was the elemental getting bigger? Or was Jay shrinking?

"Brina," he whispered, trying to warn.

"You tried to name her and tried to own her," the elemental said, *"but the shell you possessed was meaningless."*

"The same shell you possess now?" Brina asked, tilting her head as if confused. "Is the *sakkri* even in there with you? Did you protect her at all, or did you just claim her for your own use? After all, you could not have been too fond of her, considering you were the one who gave her away. Is all this anger just a mask for your own regrets?"

Brina's distraction had given Jay a chance to recall their original plan: get inside Shantel land, and therefore inside the elemental's defenses, so Leona could fight back. *If the Shantel elemental is here, where's Leona?*

"You think this is all of me?" the elemental replied to his thought. *"This shell you see is a fragment of my power, nothing more*

than I need to speak with you. The battle continues, beyond the ken of mere mortals."

"Shantel!" Xeke called, striding forward. "This is a foolish battle."

The elemental turned to him, and the felines moved closer, snarling, until the rumble of the earth threw Jay and Brina to the ground. Only as he fell did Jay realize that Xeke's form was shimmering, as overwhelming to behold as the possessed *sakkri* herself.

One of Xeke's progenitors has a bond to an earth elemental called Leshan, Rikai had said. *I was able to partially block Xeke's connection to Leona and tighten his bond to Leshan.*

By bringing Xeke into this place, they had allowed more than just a vampire to breach the Shantel's defenses.

"Leshan," Shantel demanded. *"Why have you ridden your bond into my territory?"*

"Shantel," Xeke replied, his voice deeper now, his form changing to the golden and green of summer trees. *"This bond's body is fading. I can preserve him for a time, but not the way Leona could. He will die. In that way, you have killed many of my bonds. Did you expect me not to respond?"*

"I have meddled with no one not tainted by the fire," Shantel replied. The cats near her raised their hackles.

"We have had a truce with Leona for millennia," Xeke—or Leshan now—said. *"You know this!"*

"Truce?" The day became darker as the forest canopy inexplicably thickened, covering the Shantel courtyard. *"That truce ended when my* sakkri *was destroyed by those bound to Leona—and*

you, *Leshan, among others. Jeshickah's trainers fed many of you, didn't they? Fed you in the flesh and blood of* my *people!*"

Out of the forests came serpents with bodies of sand and jaguars whose heavy footfalls left behind smoldering ash. From the canopy came birds made of vibrating light, brilliant against the darkening night sky, their wings making a crystalline ringing sound as they struck the air. Looking at them made Jay's eyes water and his body ache. When he finally forced himself to turn away, he saw that Rikai too had changed in the last few minutes. Jay wasn't certain what power had ridden her into this place, but it made every hair on the back of his neck rise. Earth, air, fire, and water were neutral elemental powers. The one Rikai had brought was mad and dark and hungry.

Her oil-slick eyes had become vortexes. In a voice like nothing he had ever heard, she said to him, "You want to run now."

Jay grabbed Brina's hand and called to Lynx, and they nearly flew over the wall. Behind them, he felt heat and concussion as the immortal powers collided. He could hear the hiss of snow vaporizing and—

Brina screamed as they stumbled into a solid mass of branches.

Can't go that way, he thought to her.

They turned, but they both knew the truth; the forest was trying to hold them here.

"*Shantel has bonded itself to you,*" a voice on the wind said. One of the other elementals had diverted its attention enough to speak to them. "*When it keeps you close, it is stronger. You must get out so we can contain it. Get far away–back to your home, if you can. From neutral ground, you can summon Shantel. You are not strong enough to bind it to your will, but if you call to us as well, we will assist you."*

How?

There was a long hesitation, and a mournful cry.

"Betrayal to tell you this," the voice said, *"but there is no other choice."*

What followed was not words but an expression of power. Within the power was a name—one that mortal vocal cords could never utter aloud, for it was the true name of one of the immortals. With this name, the immortal could be commanded if one's will was strong enough. And then came knowledge of the ritual they needed to perform.

"Why would you help us?" Jay gasped as he ran, wary of making yet more deals with immortal beings. No, that wasn't the right question. "Why do *you* need *us* to help you fight? We're just mortal."

"Shantel has crippled us all through its sly feeding all these years, and now it would destroy us in its mad quest for impossible vengeance," the elemental replied. *"We are too weak to overpower it unless it is summoned and bound."*

"But—"

"I do not know what this will do to you," the power warned. *"Such binding is unpredictable. The ritual could drain the power from every creature in your circle, or grant them immortal life . . . or grant them immortal hunger. There is no way of knowing until it is done. But it must be done. Now go!"*

The wind shoved hard at their backs, blowing shards of stone and earth at them and nearly knocking Jay off his feet.

This way! Lynx yowled at them. *No, no, not there. Close your eyes, humans,* Lynx howled. *Ignore these illusions. Follow me. Trust me.*

Jay closed his eyes without hesitation. Brina, too, shut hers and threw her senses into the lynx.

Blindly, they ran. Cold and exhausted, they forced their bodies to move, and keep moving.

At times they fell, and their bodies slept deeply. Lynx commanded Jay's power to keep them from freezing.

When at last they stumbled out of the woods, they could do nothing more than climb into the car. Too exhausted to drive, Jay dialed his phone with trembling hands and begged someone from the closest SingleEarth to pick them up and arrange for the fastest transport possible back to Haven #2.

Then they slept, but could not rest, because their dreams were still twined with the elementals' thoughts, and they both dreamed of the ongoing battle.

They wept as they saw what was happening to the world around them. An off-season hurricane. Abrupt, unexpected blizzards, dropping snow and sleet and hail and freezing rain. In another area, wildfire. A volcano came to life, rumbling out of its centuries of sleep. As the earth shook, buildings tumbled.

These poor creatures, Brina thought. *So helpless, so frightened.*

Jay needed to hold her. She let him, and they continued to sleep.

CHAPTER 26

"WE'RE AT NUMBER Two," an exhausted human voice said, rousing Brina, who was still wrapped in Jay's arms. She hadn't wanted to let go of him as they had stumbled, semi-conscious, from a car to a plane to another car, with people asking desperate questions but finally just accepting Jay's often-repeated statement that they had to get back to Haven #2.

What Brina had seen in her nocturnal visions swept over her and dragged a sob from her throat. Thousands—no, *hundreds* of thousands—of humans must have died in the last twenty-four hours. Those who believed called to their gods for explanations and help.

The humans were not alone.

Some of Leona's bonds had succumbed to the siphoning

away of their power, or to human ailments such as pneumonia, or to physical frailties such as heart attack and stroke. Some of the other elementals that had come to fight Shantel were trying to support Leona's damaged bonds, but they could do only so much.

Jay stirred with a moan, and then pushed himself up, groping for the car door handle so groggily that they both nearly fell when it opened.

"We need a blade," Brina said. She remembered everything the powers in the forest had told them, and she did not intend to hesitate.

She saw Jay seeking out specific faces in the crowd, but neither delayed their task. They both snapped commands to nurses and secretaries. Shouting over the protests, they had the ill in the gymnasium moved, until the group could form a rough circle around the outside of the room.

"Take hands," Jay said to those surrounding him—sick and well, human, witch, and shapeshifter alike. "If the person you are next to cannot grip, then hold on to them as tightly as you can. We *cannot* break the circle. Is that understood?"

Jeremy looked up with bleary eyes as he took the hands of those beside him. "Jay . . . what are we doing?"

"Saving us all," Jay answered.

"Possibly dooming us all," Brina added more honestly.

There was no choice, and no time to explain the danger. *The ritual could drain the power from every creature in your circle, or grant them immortal life . . . or grant them immortal hunger.*

Jay quashed the protest from his conscience that there *was* enough time to say a few words of warning. With so much at stake, he couldn't afford to give people a chance to refuse. He kept silent.

Brina and Jay walked to the circle's center carrying their tools.

Each element required a different form of sacrifice to call it. Water asked for tears. Air was called through breath and voice. Fire answered only to blood. Earth, like the power of the Shantel, was bound in flesh.

Brina needed only to remember what she had recently seen, and the tears ran down her face. She further recalled her brother's destruction, and well before that, the blackening bodies of each of her family. The end of safety in her world. She did not know what memories Jay pulled upon, but she did not need to. When their eyes met, the witch's were glistening.

She felt the world shift around them, wavering as power responded to their wordless command for attention.

Invoking air at that moment was more challenging, because Brina's throat was still tight with tears. She choked on her first attempt to draw breath, and so it was Jay who began with a traditional folk tune. It didn't matter what the words were, though Jay had chosen a tune of longing and loss. It mattered only that their voices mingled in the air.

Jay passed Brina his blade, clenching his jaw as Shantel's power within him fought against Leona's power embedded in the silver. He held up his arm, and Brina drew a line of blood across the palm of his hand; he took the knife and did the same for her.

Normally, a sorcerer willing to risk life and soul might have summoned one elemental, in an attempt to dominate it and win incredible power. But no trained sorcerer was foolish enough to invite this many forces into their circle at once. They would tear each other—and the mortal arrogant enough to summon them—to shreds.

In this case, that was the point. The other elementals were the weapons Jay and Brina needed to wield.

"Only one guest left to invite," Jay muttered to Brina, his voice wavering with nerves.

The name the elemental had spoken to her, Brina uttered now, not with breath but with the power gathered within the circle. She whispered it as a prayer and screamed it as a demand simultaneously, and as she did so, she reached for Jay, drew him close, and kissed him.

Their bloody hands twined, pressure stopping the blood's flow, and the kiss cut both of their voices off, leaving only the original mortal power: the touch of flesh to flesh.

It was the power that passed between mother and infant when she held her child for the first time. It was the power of a gentle touch to the cheek, a reassuring pat on the shoulder, a sympathetic hug—or an angry slap. Every human being knew the power that arose when flesh met flesh.

Brina could have just held on to Jay, leaned her cheek against his, and used that contact for the leverage she needed to summon the Shantel elemental. They needed only to invoke it, not to provide the kind of sacrifice that would have been necessary to call it the first time. She chose this because she had wanted to kiss him since sometime in the forest.

Jay, though surprised, responded as she had hoped he would—willingly, with the same memories of shared experiences and an understanding of all the beauty and agony they had both endured recently.

The power that passed between them was sweet, and gentle, and the opposite of everything the Shantel had fed on for the last two centuries. It was a reminder of what had been, and what could be again. It drew Shantel close, until the circle around them shuddered with the elemental's appearance, hands clutching hands in the effort to contain the power.

The power of flesh could be compassion and forgiveness— but not this time. Shantel would find no absolution here. Too many lives had been lost, and neither Jay nor Brina was the turn-the-other-cheek type. The other elementals who had stepped into the circle around them, some claiming bodies too worn down by disease to even open their eyes on their own, were also not the types to let the matter be forgotten.

As one they struck.

The circle constricted, creating a noose that strangled the Shantel elemental, siphoning its power away.

Brina could have interfered. She and Jay had summoned the elemental. They could have commanded the others to leave it; they could have claimed its power for themselves.

And such power it would have been!

I'm sorry, Brina said to it. Not just for the horrors of Midnight; that was not what had truly undone this elemental. She was apologizing for keeping away from the Shantel the one person who had been able to speak to it, and hear its voice, and let it be truly alive. Without its *sakkri*, it had been voiceless and helpless.

The Shantel elemental buckled, unraveling. Other elementals stole its memories, all the thoughts that gave it form, ripping them away like children tearing paper off Christmas presents.

Jay and Brina both collapsed to their knees as those memories lashed at them, seeking new homes. They accepted the ones they wanted, some beautiful and some terrible, some as ancient as the land itself and some as recent as Brina's trying to hang herself from the rafters and Pet struggling for hours with the knowledge that her mistress had not given her any orders regarding cutting her down, but surely she couldn't intend to stay that way forever. . . .

That which was immortal could not die. But without mortal memories to hold it together, it could not maintain its consciousness.

Brina whispered the Shantel's name once again, but received no response. The entity had been reduced to a mere child of its kind, barely sentient, with no recollection of what it had just done.

It had no physical form in the room, but she could sense it, and she knew it rested deeply.

"It's over?" Jay asked, looking up, his expression as dazed as Brina felt.

One of the ill spoke up—no, this being was beyond ill. Brina knew that the human form she was looking at was deceased, though it had been appropriated by one of the elementals.

"*Leona has been injured. Weakened,*" it said. "*She cannot hold all of her bonds any more. Many will die yet.*" A wail arose from somewhere in the crowd, before the elemental added, "*Unless they are willing to make other arrangements.*"

"*We can pick up the slack, so to speak,*" another voice said. This elemental was gentler, but Brina knew it was hungry as well.

Jay started to speak. "My family—"

"*We are grateful for your help. Looking after your kin is the least we can do,*" one of the voices offered, before another swiftly interjected, "*Leona's mortal children are numerous, of course. It may take more than one of us to save them.*"

Some of the voices sounded kind; the last one just sounded sly. Leona had been the most powerful of the elementals. Now she had been laid low, and though other elementals had saved her, they did not plan to let her regain the same level of power ever again. That meant claiming her weakened bonds as their own. It would save lives—if it wasn't too late—but this world was never going to be the same again.

Brina looked at Jay, wondering whether the new world painted this day would be better than the one before, or even the one that would have resulted had they not interfered with Shantel's plans. He heard the thought, pondered, and then said, "I need a nap."

Brina nodded. Others could clean up the mess left behind . . . whatever was left behind. They had done their job.

CHAPTER 27

JAY COULD NOT rest until he had made several phone calls ensuring that those he loved were still alive. Some were in critical condition, but if there was a spark of life left within them, he trusted the elementals to save them.

For their own purposes, perhaps, but the elementals would save them nonetheless.

Next, he decided to sleep for a week. Unfortunately, the rest of the world insisted on getting in the way of this triumphant hero's nap—including Brina, who he had thought would be on his side.

She shook him and demanded he stand up because she wanted a model *right now*. He had no idea where she had found the materials. When he looked up with every intention of telling her to come back in another seven days, he had the irresistible desire to kiss her instead. So he did. And then he modeled.

Brina painted in a new way. She used her brushes and her oils—with windows open despite the frigid winter air—but occasionally she reached for the canvas and caressed it, sliding fingers over wet or dry paint. The image would shift, lines and tones responding to the pictures in her head in a way that normal paint could not.

Strangely, she was neither disturbed by this development nor delighted. She merely considered it a new tool, one she was happy to get to know, but she never questioned it. Jay would say that she took it for granted, but he might as well have said that she took *everything* for granted.

For Brina, each moment was new, as it is, and perfect.

Unfortunately, she wasn't the only one asking for his time. Some of the people who insisted on bothering him brought good things, like food. Others *wanted* things from him.

Jay, what's going on? Jay, our magic is doing odd things. Jay, so-and-so has recovered from the flu but now keeps shapeshifting into a chicken.

Okay, he hadn't heard the bit about the chicken *specifically*, but there had been reports of unexpected shapeshifting, especially among those who had been in the circle when the elementals had been summoned. Powers that people had long controlled were gone, but others spontaneously manifested. Some of those new powers were gifts. Some were darker, ranging from empathy like Jay's—but without a lifetime to learn

how to use it or control it—to power over life and death, healing's inverse.

Individuals who before had only needed to eat as humans
did found themselves needing to *feed,* while others who had
fed on blood or power for centuries now had entirely different
hungers.

The world had changed. Jay still didn't know how many
of Midnight's trainers and traders had survived. Most of the
vampires he knew had no interest in updating him, and having
just barely saved the world from his last series of best intentions, Jay believed that it might be best to let this sleeping dog
lie. For now.

He had other priorities.

Jay stood next to Jeremy as the groom waited, struggling
not to fidget or wipe his sweaty palms on his tuxedo pants.
Something to do with saving the world, or at least Caryn's
life, or maybe just the super-flu leaving much of the original
wedding party feeling under the weather, had caused them to
promote Jay from usher to groomsman.

The human looked good—though, these days, *human* might
not have been the most accurate word. Jeremy had been born
human, but he had also been in the circle when the Shantel
elemental had been summoned. No one knew quite what had
touched the doctor-in-training, but Jay knew Jeremy's eyes had
a phosphorescence visible when the room was dark, and he
tended not to notice anymore when no lights were on. So far,
that was the extent of his manifested power; maybe that was all
there would be.

Whatever he was, Jeremy could still sweat. He looked to Jay anxiously. He had all the faith in the world that Caryn would appear and walk down that aisle . . . but what if she didn't? What if she had changed her mind? What if she was . . .

The music rose. Caryn had chosen "Colors of the Wind" as her wedding march.

It was beautiful; the bride was beautiful.

Jay barely managed not to laugh out loud as Brina's idle thought reached him: *So provincial, so traditional. Nothing original. Beautiful dress, but portraits of brides in their beautiful dresses are a dime a dozen.*

Her mind went back to wandering more interesting paths. In the last days, Brina had not regained her vampirism. Jay knew she had considered contacting Kaleo, the one who had changed her nearly four hundred years ago, though she had not spoken of it out loud. She hadn't decided what she planned to do. At Jay's prompting, she had called Nikolas and officially given him permission to take charge of all her "property," to do with as he saw fit. SingleEarth had accepted several of the slaves into their psychiatric rehabilitation program.

She was getting used to taking care of herself, and being independent, just as she was getting used to her heartbeat, and her breath.

Jay was getting used to her primal, childlike joy. They had taken a break from painting once when Brina had needed fresh air, and she had followed him, running through the forest, de-lighted by the falling dust of snow. With Lynx by their side, they had leapt, tumbled into snowbanks, and reveled in the crispness of nature.

Jay fervently hoped she didn't choose to become a vampire again.

Especially since he was pretty sure she had the makings of a powerful witch.

It had taken Jay's kind many millennia to develop their powers into what they were these days—the Vidas with their ability to manipulate raw power, the Smoke line's ability to heal, and all the other specialties Jay knew only a little of. Now they were all back at the beginning again. None of them knew what they were or who they might be in coming generations.

Jeremy and Caryn—would they be the parents of a new line of witches? Or of something else entirely? For that matter, what might Jay's children be, if he chose to have children?

At that moment, all that mattered was the way the crystals on Caryn's gown sparkled in the light, wreathing her in rainbows. It wasn't a strange new power that gave her such a glow—no, it was love, and hope, and relief, and joy.

She smiled up at her husband-to-be with absolutely no concern about what Jeremy might be or might become. It didn't matter to her. She knew who he was. Who cared what he was?

His parents cared, more than a little. A few people in the audience were simmering with resentment and built-up anger that Jay suspected might lead to a fistfight in the lobby during the reception.

Jay tried to come up with a plan to defuse the potential mayhem. After all, Jeremy had given him this job because he had unique talents that were supposed to help him avoid bloodshed over the wedding cake.

"Do you have the rings?"

Oh—and that!

Jay did have the rings. He passed them to Jeremy, and then there wasn't much more for Jay to do except stand there and look interested while letting his mind wander across the thoughts of all those assembled.

It was amazing how few of them were thinking about the recent illness, or all the loss, or their fears of the future. All their thoughts were on this day, this moment, as Jeremy and Caryn leaned toward each other to kiss. . . .

Meanwhile, in a small but elite penthouse bar in New York City . . .

Kaleo and Theron leaned back and watched fireworks from the balcony. No disaster could keep humans down long, it seemed.

"I knew a Malinalxochitl witch once, but I never had the magic myself," Theron commented. "The Azteka were mostly after my time. So why do I suddenly find myself doing things like this?"

He glanced at the candle flickering at the center of the table. Theron held up a hand, and the tiny ball of flame came to his palm like an obedient puppy. With a flick of his wrist he juggled it to the other hand, and then sent it back to the candle, where it flared at least three feet high before settling back to its normal and natural state.

Kaleo watched the display and shook his head. "I'm sure you will make good use of this new talent. It is more useful than some of the aberrations that have come to my attention."

"I've heard the rumors, of course," Theron said. "I'm looking into them, and trying to determine which of the wild speculations is most correct. So far, most of what I've heard has been barely credible, and some of it has been outright impossible . . . like vampires turning human."

Kaleo nodded, his gaze going distant. "Indeed."

"I heard about Brina," Theron said. "What are you planning to do?"

"Legally, I suppose she's mine, since she was before the change. I would appreciate it if you could help me spread the word that I will enforce that claim, should anyone attempt to harm her."

"Do you intend to bring her in?"

"No, I think not," Kaleo said thoughtfully. "I killed her once, and discovered then that she is a very different woman as one of us than she was as a mortal."

"She'll die," Theron pointed out.

"Nothing beautiful lasts forever."

And in the heart of New Mayhem . . .

Fala stared at the corpse in front of her as it rapidly deteriorated. It wasn't rotting; she knew what it looked like when a body rotted. This one was decaying in a different way, like a mummy in dry sand.

Moira and Jager had both been unconscious, wrapped in wild dreams, for days. Fala had drawn on magic in order to sustain them, magic she had barely used since she was a human sorcerer. When they had woken, the three of them had hunted like wild animals, desperate to renew their strength. They had barely survived.

Apparently, some others had not.

The body in front of Fala, which she suspected would be dust within days, was wearing one of Silver's thousand-dollar suits. It was also in his office.

Should she do something for him? Maybe she could bring a mortal in here, slit its throat over the body, and see if the cascade of blood would revive the decomposing ancient.

She kicked it instead, sending debris flying like ash into the air and causing the body to crumble further. That way, she didn't have to wonder whether or not he would wake up.

She went looking for Aubrey, to see if he had survived this cataclysm. Given her bad luck, he probably had. It seemed like the younger vampires had fared better. Moira had been in better shape than Jager; Aubrey was younger than Moira by about five centuries. Sadly, he was probably fine.

And in a small town in Maryland . . .

Kyla leant her shoulder to clearing wreckage from what had, a few days before, been the entrance to the Dragon's Nest club. More recently, it had been a sick ward for serpiente who had fallen ill, including Kyla's brother, Lucien Cobriana.

Somewhere in the worst of the fever, Lucien had started raving in the ancient language, too rapidly for Kyla to follow with her limited understanding of the tongue and the fever filling her own brain. It had sounded like he was arguing with someone.

Then the ground had started to shake, as if the earth itself were shivering. Lucien had opened eyes that were no longer just the rust-red of cobra eyes but that had burned like liquid magma. He had grabbed her arm. Dragged her up. Shoved her to the door, and commanded, *"Run!"*

He had evacuated most of the serpents in the nest, but when the ground had collapsed, it had swallowed him. Kyla hadn't been able to inform the rest of the family, because no one had been able to reach *anyone* else in the serpiente royal house. All she could do was supervise the rescue attempt, and pray.

And in the Le Coire manor . . .

"Are you ever going to tell us what the hell that was all about?" Brent asked.

"Once I fully understand it, and know what I am allowed to tell you, I will consider whether or not I want to bother," Ryan replied.

Samantha sighed. It had been a difficult few weeks. She knew that whatever had happened had involved others of her kind, but she hadn't had enough power to participate in the fight . . . or to even know who was fighting, or over what, or who had won.

Ryan had only come downstairs to eat. Otherwise, they hadn't seen him in days; he had been sequestered in his private ritual area, trying to communicate with the ancient powers to which his family had long ago tied themselves.

All he had reported so far was that there had been a major shift in power globally. No one currently in the room had been seriously affected, but word on the street was that many things had changed.

And in a coffee shop in Boston . . .

The three known as the Wild Cards sat around the same table where they often gathered to chat.

Rikai's skin had returned to its flawlessly smooth porcelain, the scars hidden, and her muscles and joints were once again functioning as they had before the Inquisitors had treated her to the third degree. The elemental that had ridden her had been one she was already familiar with, a creature not of one of the pure elements—fire, earth, water, and air—but of agony and rage.

Xeke had fed once since they had returned from the forest, but it had been mostly out of habit. He suspected he didn't need blood anymore. The power given to him by the elemental had shifted his needs. Thankfully, he had plenty of mortals willing to stay near him and sleep in his arms, keeping the power well fed and content . . . and he could still appreciate a macchiato, which this particular café made very well.

Renna leaned back and enjoyed her chai latte, already contemplating who she would choose as her narrator. As always, the others had been involved in forming the story, and she was left to write it.

Her power had changed, she thought, but who could really tell? She had been born an Arun witch, tainted by vampires, partially trained as a Triste, and now possessed more than one strain of shapeshifter power. All of that had been jumbled and reassembled. It would be fun to see what happened next.

She pulled out her laptop, flipped it open, and opened her word processor.

"I think the best place to start would be at Kendra's Heathen Holiday," Xeke said. "With Jay coming in from the snow."

Renna nodded. She had visited the gala briefly, but too many people didn't like her, mostly due to her propensity to tell the stories she learned, regardless of the preferences of those involved. But she knew how things had looked. She knew that Daryl's *Lady with a Falcon on Her Fist* had stood in the front hall this year; Xeke had already told her how it had stopped Jay cold as he'd examined it, as if unsure whether he could love it for its beauty or should hate it for its creator.

Yes, she would begin there.

ABOUT THE AUTHOR

AMELIA ATWATER-RHODES wrote her first novel, *In the Forests of the Night*, when she was thirteen. Other books in the Den of Shadows series are *Demon in My View*, *Shattered Mirror*, *Midnight Predator*, *Persistence of Memory*, *Token of Darkness*, and *All Just Glass*. She has also written the five-volume series The Kiesha'ra: *Hawksong*, a *School Library Journal* Best Book of the Year and a Voice of Youth Advocates Best Science Fiction, Fantasy, and Horror Selection; *Snakecharm*; *Falcondance*; *Wolfcry*, an IRA-CBC Young Adults' Choice; and *Wyvernhail*. *Poison Tree* is her most recent novel. Visit her online at AmeliaAtwaterRhodes.com.